THOMAS KABDEBO

TRACKING GIORGIONE

BRANDON

First published in Britain and Ireland in 2009 by Brandon
an imprint of Mount Eagle Publications
Dingle, Co. Kerry, Ireland, and
Unit 3, Olympia Trading Estate, Coburg Road, London N22 6TZ, England

www.brandonbooks.com

ISBN 9780863223945

Supported by the Péterfy Foundation of the Hungarian Union of Writers

2 4 6 8 10 9 7 5 3 1

Mount Eagle Publications receives support from
the Arts Council/An Chomhairle Ealaíon.

Cover design: Anú Design
Typesetting by Red Barn Publishing, Skeagh, Skibbereen
Printed in the UK

To D. + L. + M. + K.
and the memory of H.

(There may not be any other lasting triumph
than that of Art—all others are pyrrhic)

Pre Position

O ur knowledge and our perception of it increases as we talk.
I'll give you my summary: when we see a picture in colour
which we can also identify, then a large part of our brain is
mobilised. The picture itself is customised in the mind by the
unification of dots or points of up to a million or more. Let us
say that the mind has a virtual screen where the picture—
through the channels starting from the eye—appears. I imagine tiny pieces of a Lego construction: the mind connects these
points in two ways. It interprets the image, and links it up with
other images. Take *Judith*, by Giorgione, with the head of
Holofernes in the Hermitage Museum in Leningrad. This may
bring to the informed mind other representations of the same
biblical event by other painters. Furthermore, it links the cut-
off head of Holofernes to others of the same ilk, such as
Goliath's head or the head of John the Baptist (usually carried
on a tray) in the *Court of Herod*. But it may also speak to other
senses by connecting to *ferosons*—stimulants. Judith's exquisite
left leg, much in the foreground, may be seen as appealing to
the male sex. The picture (any picture) may mobilise body func-
tions: we may glow, perspire, smile or get angry, feel an inspiration to act in a certain way: e.g. copy the picture, write about

it or, in extreme cases, tear up the original (the Savonarola effect). The picture also involves our aesthetic judgement: we like or dislike the image, we discover puzzles in its structure or reorganisation, as in Salvador Dalí; it usually expands our knowledge of the painter, his range, his technique, his choice of subject. We may classify the painting itself in our own list of masters, we may increase our knowledge—after seeing it—in terms of forms, colours and composition.

The mind is capable of constructing a map where the observed picture is a focal point of crossroads. Most pictures have a life-enhancing quality as you enter into a different world from your own. Some pictures, on the other hand, conjure up the cemetery of the mind: they disgust, revolt, upset our sense of values. Mind control also works with pictures: it concentrates us on forceful images, and on other matters. Some pictures create in the mind a patch of positive or negative puzzle. The Baptist's head makes us wonder at justice and reward; *The Tempest*, by Giorgione, makes us wonder what the meaning of this fabulous assemblage might be.

(from the notebook of Giorgio Barbatella)

1. Anabasis

"There is no ending to any story, only a curtailed new beginning."
(Alessandro Manzoni)

Sunday, 5 December 2004, was the eve of my fortieth birthday and the namesday of St Nicholas of Bohemia, whom the Czechs call Mikulás. I know a bit about him since my mother, Francesca, keeps an account of the most significant saints of the Church, and since my wife, Helena, is Czech herself. My mother lay great store on San Niccolò being my spiritual godfather, the real one being Don Ignazio, a priest serving in Brompton Oratory, who also willingly deprived me, *bebe Barbatella,* of my pagan status and from the original sin we were all born with. There was a friendly disagreement between my mother and father—I was told about it a good deal later—regarding my Christian names. My mother, in honour of San Niccolò, wanted to give me the respectable name of Nicholas soon after the hours of her labour and just after my birth at 7 A.M., but my father insisted on the name George or Giorgio, who was, after all, another saint (his existence not yet doubted), the one who represented England (my family's adopted home) and was his own Christian name too.

"*Litigerano*" (they quarrelled gently), related Don Ignazio, on my tenth name day, for it was the custom in my family to

celebrate name days as well as birthdays, with modest gifts and humble festivities, apart from the munificent Christmases, Easters and my parents' wedding anniversaries. This last date was August 1 of any year, and it took me a good while (when a teenager) to discover and realise that they married in 1964 only four months before my birth. This had puzzled me for a while—I would say even disturbed me—before I summoned courage, and asked my mother.

"Ask your dad," said she.

Well, back to the Christian names. They agreed to give me two of them: George and Nicholas. The same friends who called my dad "*maggiore*" decided to call me "*minore*" until, at the age of sixteen, these epithets became laughable. Dad was 5' 9", not too tall, but robustly built, while I twigged up to 6 foot exactly. I remained the same as the years went by, but I grew in strength and developed the same muscle-filled arms and legs as Dad had. It is only now at the age of seventy-five that he has begun to shrink slightly and to find digging the soil tiring. Hence his official retirement.

We were living in Woodlawn Road, Fulham, a mile-long road of London SW6, which is parallel with Craven Cottage, home to many triumphs, and even more failures, of Fulham Football Club. Dad was a faithful supporter of the club—still is, although he cannot stand Harrods' boss, the owner, the chairman, the *totum factum* of FFC. As long as I remember, we attended the home matches on alternate Saturdays, stamping our feet on the stands in the first two decades, and then sitting on grandstand seats afterwards, since the rebirth of Fulham FC. This club, friendly, and capable of lovely surprises, remains in the centre of my heart, while for Dad it was verily a convenient substitute. He was a Juventus fan, a born Juve aficionado, as behoves a young male who hailed form the north of Italy.

"Mark my word, son, Fulham will never win a European trophy, not even an English one," said he in one of his rare pronouncements. He was nearly proved wrong twice: once Fulham got near to winning the League Cup, then almost bagged the FA Cup on another occasion. As a sapling I was sent to train with other saplings at Craven Cottage. I was not altogether talentless but not exactly gifted either. From the dilemma of to play or not to play (*giocare o non giocare*), I was liberated by the arrival of Zio Giuseppe (Uncle Joe) from Rome, with his City of Rome fencing team.

The day of St Nicholas, 6 December. As always on 6 December, I received a small gift from Mamma: "You know, this is your second name day, and San Niccolò was generous to children."

The gift was a chocolate Santa, made in Milan of dark chocolate with generous cocoa content, my favourite. I am now over forty and Mum still treats me as a child, and occasionally calls me Niccolò. According to Helena, Czech cultural history knows two Mikuláš. One was an early medieval saint, a bishop, nearly as poor as those children to whom he gave everything he ever had (a kind of St Philip of Neri of Rome, or a holy version of Robin Hood). The Czech Mikuláš also had a hood; Helena drew him once and coloured his figure deep red. The second Mikuláš lived in the nineteenth century and behaved *deliberately* like his predecessor. He was good by imitation. The first one had a traditional white beard. Later, in his cultural role he merged with Santa, while the second one had a real beard, his early photographs appearing in a magazine.

Helena said: "The fusion, or the merger of Mikuláš and

Santa (of Christmas) was only extended to some countries; in other lands, such as Slovakia, Bohemia or Hungary, Mikuláš had kept his identity and his date: 6 December. The Christmas gifts, delivered either by the Christmas Angel or by Jesus Christ himself, are now part of the Christmas Eve customs or Christmas Day customs, or St Stephen's Day/Boxing Day customs."

And who is the Jewish Santa or Islam's Mikuláš, or the Buddhist Father Christmas, I wonder.

Since then I've learned that the Japanese have their Winter Father, and the Chinese too. During the iron curtain years, eastern European countries had undergone a change: their Santa was pronounced clerical, therefore undesirable by the authorities, so he was substituted by Old-Man-Winter.

7 December

I was born in London in (what everybody calls) Hammersmith Hospital. The story is told and retold by Mother at birthdays. Dad usually sits by reading his paper, smoking an occasional cigarette or looking at the TV. I am summoned by Mamma, and asked to sit down on the stool by her feet, clad in furry slippers. The fur is worn, the soles are patched up by Dad, who had given her the pair at their first Christmas in 1964. I was then four weeks old.

"We had no central heating in the flat,.or for that matter, in the house either; we kept warm by stoking the fire at the fireplace."

"You still have a fireplace."

Mamma: "*Zitto* (hush). Of course we have it. Nothing replaces the living fire. At the most we complement its crackling warmth by the breath of the radiator. As I was saying, I went to bed late at night. The previous night he did not sleep in a matrimonial bed, Giorgio slept in the next room. He still does. And I still love him, just the same."

Dad pricked up his ears: "Love is grand. What do we have for supper?"

"*Cacciatiore, con polenta.*"

"*Bene. Continuare, cara.*"

Although I am recording what went on, what goes on, whatever is going to be related is mainly in English; my parents' conversation is usually in standard Italian—which I understand, and speak better than a kitchen hand. When spoken to in a Veneto dialect, I can only guess at it. Their little secrets were always transmitted to one another in Veneto which I have never bothered to learn comprehensively.

"*Insomma.* At around midnight the pangs of pain woke me up, I woke your dad, he ran down the street to ring for an ambulance. We had no telephone. They took about an hour to come although the hospital was just down the road. The building is grand now, sparkling everywhere, in and outside the maternity unit which now has at least a hundred beds. At that time it couldn't have had more than twenty-five. And the beds were all occupied. First they just put me on a trolley, in a cubicle, a fat tall nurse attending to me; later they rearranged a ward, my bed was pushed near the window. Then I was separated from the others and was put into the birth room, visited by the obstetrician. I waited, and waited, and waited. The doctor, a podgy little man with podgy little hands, bespectacled, came. Giorgio sat outside in the corridor. The husband's attendance at birth was not yet encouraged in those days. Between the attacks of pain, caused by your son" (she nodded towards Dad) "wanting vehemently to come out, I was attempting to understand the reason for your very early coming." (She patted my hand.) "We were expecting a postnatal *Natale*, a baby to be born at Christmas, or the New Year—even at Epiphany, at the latest—but you were so anxious to see this world of hustle and bustle, this world of woes and shadows, that you came on the morn of San Niccolò; I felt sick. They gave me an emetic, which made me more sick. Then I felt I was going to burst. The doc gave me an epidural; it helped the pain, not the tension. Then: crunch. I yelled so loudly that Giorgio came in from the corridor. The nurse kindly showed him out. After the crunch: NIAGARA. The water flowed like the biblical flood. Clean sailing now. Soon your head appeared, the doc got hold of it, pulled out the rest of you, and put you, lock-stock-and-barrel (blood, guts and mucous) on my chest. You were small, purple, large-headed, with under-developed limbs, whimpering, instead of crying, under-developed, and undersize. Not more than thirty centimetres long."

"More than a foot, he was. And that is thirty-one and a half centimetres."

"*Bene, bene.* A foot then. Yet altogether a miserable looking . . ."

"Two days in intensive care, where he learned to suck from the bottle . . ."

"Then he began to milk me, and soon to suck me dry . . . And look at him now! The ugliness has disappeared, the ugly duckling has changed into a swan." (She kissed me affectionately.)

"Signor Andersen, or whoever he was, he got it wrong. It is the gosling that turns into a swan. A nearer relative of the swan rather than the duckling."

"Gaggle, gaggle," I said.

"Broad shouldered, barrel chested, brown, handsome boy."
She ruffled my hair.

"Your dad's dark wavy hair, my one-time bronze crown mellowed into your walnut-coloured hair. My delicate white skin, and your father's sallow complexion produced, in fusion, this ever-so-lightly hued off-white colour on your strong limbs. And your face. *La faccia*! I can see his brown eyes, my full lips, his strong chin, my high cheekbones in you, son."

"You are not praising the nose, Francesca. It is flat."

"Giorgino. The boy could not help that. The knuckleduster in an urchin's hand broke his nose. But that was later."

Indeed, when I look into a mirror—strictly during shaving—a boxer's face looks back at me. We were sixteen. (Ali has preserved his face but not his wits.) Parson's Green grammar school, which I attended by spanning the twice two miles distance from Woodlawn Road and back on my bike had a mixed bunch of sixth formers. One day I took out a girl I'd particularly fancied, the one with the bewitching one green and one blue eye. But she had other admirers. A fellow called MacDermot—was he Scottish or Northern Irish?—smaller but more aggressive than me, and equipped with an iron knuckleduster, attacked me after school and broke my nose irretrievably. Oh yes, in return, and with blood gushing out my nostrils, he got a good hiding from me. But my once regular nose was flattened, and remained out of joint even after it had healed. The incident made me cautious with girls, and with rivals. Moderately so.

As I recall my childhood and early boyhood, my parents were always working hard. My dad was employed by the Bishop of London, so to speak; he was a gardener in Bishop's Park. His days of nine to five were peppered with private commissions.

He created private gardens by invitation, first in Fulham, our district, then in Chelsea or over the Thames in Putney. He would not take a job further than that because, for many years, he was just riding a pushbike, and only from the mid-Seventies a small van that could accommodate the three of us, and pots and plants and fertilisers and garden tools in the back. I have no sisters and brothers. Only when I grew up was I told that my mother had sustained an infection, and through hysterectomy she lost her womb. Perhaps this would partly explain her excessive love of me, although—as I could see when looking around later—Italian mothers express far more affection than English mothers do. The emphasis is on the word *express,* and not on the word *affection.*

My mum was, and is, excessively house proud. As soon as we could afford it, we had parquet floors and quality rugs, some Persian. You had to take your shoes off in the hall and select a pair of slippers from the different sizes there provided. The alternatives were socks or stockings or bare feet. The windows were cleaned inside once a month by Mother and outside by Father. Spring cleaning every two months. I was taught washing up before the age of nine, and to attend to the tiny rose garden at the back soon after that. Dad had created the rose garden for their tenth anniversary, showing me how to care for the roses, how to cut, prune and feed them, provide the trellises to climb on, and how to graft, using one kind to receive another. At fifteen I succeeded in creating a blue rose.

12 December, the day of Gabriella
Three times a week Mother took the number 14 bus and travelled as far as South Kensington where she was the "alternative cook" at La Bocca restaurant. The owner, Ricardo, a Michelin

man by girth, was Venetian by birth and a distant friend of the della Croce family. This was Mother's maiden name, laden with centuries of fame, legend and pretensions of nobility. La Bocca was a quality restaurant, proudly displaying the three stars Mr Ronay had given it. The restaurant was renowned for its traditional Italian cooking, as well as for its innovations or novelties. In Mamma's three days she cooked *saltimbocca Romana* once, *ravioli con ostrighe*, and—this required no cooking only arranging—*vitello tonato*. Yet this last one was the most difficult, because only one of the so called continental butchers provided veal. Once in one quarter year or so, Mum came out with one of her special creations. Our favourite was the *stekka con fettucine e carciofi*. Any day when Mother cooked at La Bocca she was encouraged by her boss to take home a generous portion of her delectable creation for the rest of us, for supper. As this happened three times a week, she needed only four more times to cook for us. To give fresh food daily was her mania.

We frequented no other restaurant than La Bocca, where we were invited to go and dine on certain feast days. And there we met Mr Philip Long, an ardent patron of the restaurant, an Italophile gentleman with a shock of white hair and impeccable elegance. Mr Long was one of the assistant managers at Harrods in its glorious pre-Mohammed days, when it advertised itself with the slogan: *Here you can buy anything from a flea to an elephant.* At the age of fifteen I was given a holiday job there, at Easter, Christmas and summer, thanks to Mr Long. He was so delighted with my mother's cooking at La Bocca that he offered me a choice of three departments. I plumped for Arts and Crafts as my art master at school was constantly encouraging me to "develop my talents". Yes, I could draw easily enough. I made portraits, designed landscapes, illustrated the school

17

magazine and painted the school crest in acrylic. I also drew a caricature of the headmaster. At Harrods I found myself in a sea of paint of all sorts: pastel, watercolours, acrylic, chromogen oil, tex-dye inks, powder; and brushes of all sizes, easels too, ink-rollers, paint scrapers, pug mills, colour spray guns, ink-troughs. There was plaster of Paris, clay, earthenware, pottery, loan mould, glaze and God knows what else. At the end of the third year of part-time work, I received the gift of an easel from Mr Long, and in return I painted his portrait—surreptitiously, from a photograph. I framed it and delivered it to his flat in Knightsbridge. He lived in the same block as the ill-fated writer Arthur Koestler. Long was a bachelor but did not shun the company of ladies. It was a Sunday when—after a phone call—I knocked on his door carrying the portrait wrapped in brown paper. A youngish woman opened the door in a housecoat, smelling of Dior and wearing false nails.

"Philip!" she called, and I recognised her to be his secretary. I was given Strega, of which he took half a tumbler; she opted for a Bloody Mary. Long looked at his portrait with visible delight and invited me to find a place for it on the walls of any of the three rooms: the salon, the dining room and the bedroom. The last one was full of family photographs: his parents, siblings, nieces and nephews. The dining room walls were totally covered with original Piranesi illustrations, leaving not even a palmful of free space. The salon had an Italian flag, a reproduction of Michelangelo's *Tondo Pitti*, two original Chirico paintings and a reproduction of *Judith* with the head of Holofernes by Giorgione. This picture mesmerised me, the face of Judith captivated me, and my imagination began to roam around other pictures. In Judith's visage I discovered an early version of Meryl Streep's face, her slightly elongated and somewhat irregular nose—*Judith's* early sixteenth-century model might have been a Jewish colleen or an aristocratic wench, perhaps an aristo-Jewess, still innocent in her soul, yet experienced by her deed whose resolution is reflected in her face. Yet, in this biblical and historical post-killing scene, there was no aggression or triumphalism. Judith's handsome left foot is resting on Holofernes's severed head, as so many Madonnas' feet have rested on the serpent's head. Judith's face is pure poetry, the prototype of the visage of Our Lady, portrayed by Leonardo, Raphael, Dosso Dossi, Caravaggio. Mr Long waited and waited, then took his own portrait from me and hung it up in his bedroom.

13 December, Luke and Lucia
Without Luke and his Gospel, the story of Jesus would lack roundness and penetrating humanity. Without Lucia the ecclesiastical calendar would be poorer without a lovely lass who happened to be a saint. I had a maiden aunt called Lucia, just a year older than Dad. She lived in Castelfranco, and with some help, she looked after the market gardening business she had inherited from her dad, my grandfather. Her younger sister, Giuliana, now seventy years old, lived in Venice with her gondolier husband, Benedetto, in the proximity of some of her children, and grandchildren. My maternal uncle, Giuseppe della Croce, now lives in Rome, being the trainer of the *sciabolisti*, the top Roman fencing club. The London equivalent has a Hungarian trainer, Mr Károly Kovács, a one time member of the Hungarian sabre team at one of the Olympics.

We now have to row back many years. We already owned both flats in the house, purchased on two mortgage deals, and had a telephone in the upper part where we live. Now the telephone rang, and I picked up the receiver.

"*Sono Giuseppe. Zio Giuseppe. Tu sei Giorgio juniore? Non e vero?*" ("This is Giuseppe. Uncle Giuseppe. You are Giorgio junior. Isn't that right?")

"*Vero. Sono juniore.*" ("Right. I am Junior.")

"*Posso parlare con Francesca, tua mamma?*" ("May I speak with Francesca, your mamma?")

As far as I could remember, as a child, we had had no contact with either my dad's family, the Barbatella, or my mum's people, the della Croce. It was strange. We were friendly with other Italians in London, and they all seemed to maintain close family ties with their own elders. The story my mother told me went like this:

"Before you were born, we used to live in Castelfranco, a smallish town north-west of Venice. My family home, the grange, was to the north-west of the smallish town of Castelfranco. My father—your nonno—used to own quite a bit of land there. He died in the war, fighting the Germans. My mother leased the land, except a plot around the grange which she kept for gardening. Vegetable garden and flower garden with a centrepiece of a grand rockery. One day your father came along and reproduced the della Croce family crest with hyacinths, lilies and margaretas. I fell in love with him, or rather, we fell in love with one another. My mother, your nonna, was a very strict and proud lady, and sent me away to college in Padua to avoid Zorzo. I was studying domestic science. Your dad found me in Padua and visited me there as often as he could. Life in the Fifties wasn't great in Italy, so we decided to transfer to England."

Dimly, I began to put things together. "Babbo, did you get married in Italy?"

"No son, in London."

"Which church?"

"The Brompton Oratory. We knew a priest there, our parish priest of Castelfranco put us in touch with him, and it is due to him, Padre Ignazio, that we found our feet. First we rented this flat from his brother, then, as soon as we had the right deposit, bought it."

"Has he, I mean the brother, another place to live in then?"

"Rather. He is a well-to-do man, who sold us the whole house, eventually."

It took me the next ten years to realise that Mother was over four months pregnant when they crossed the channel in order to escape grandmother's wrath and the whole family's castigation. Now Giuseppe was all charm and friendliness. He had been in correspondence with Mother, secretly; Dad did not want to know the haughty della Croces who had evidently avoided and despised him. But then Giuseppe arrived, embraced him and called him *Caro Suocero* (Dear Brother-in-law). In return Dad addressed him as Don Giuseppe, which was an inch friendlier than Signor della Croce.

Helena

"Without Helen there wouldn't have been hostilities in Troy—
but no Iliad or Odyssey either."
(Tancredo Pomponazzi)

"We are created for companionship—
the gods placed our happiness in one another."
(Ienyesseb)

In my third year at the Slade school in 1984, I met a first year
student called Helena Hrabikova. She was a shy and lovely
girl, neatly dressed, who neatly painted large-postcard size pictures. She had a heart-shaped, melancholic face, often decorated with a coy smile, her eyes were brown and velvety and her
auburn hair long and finely textured. I stood behind her, facing
her easel, and watched her thin brush being dipped in aquamarine, then in bear brown and light green. The emerging picture
was a high peak in the Carpathians, which used to divide
Bohemia, then Czechoslovakia, from one-time Hungary. In the
middle of the slope there was a tiny red spot—the suggestion
of the red skirt of a girl—almost microscopic in that landscape.

"It is you," I said.

She turned her head, which sat on a swanlike neck, and
said, "How did you know?"

It took me a while to gather my wits. I watched her long

fingers holding the brush, then I dipped into the depth of her two eyes. They were shining like the sheen of a lake.

"Well, Signorina Gentileschi painted herself as Judith—the same lass who had dealt with Holofernes. Raphael put his own figure and face among the philosophers of the *School of Athens*."

She smiled again. "What comparisons. I am only an insignificant young girl, lost in the vastness of nature."

"Young, yes. Insignificant, no. For me you are the most significant person at University College."

She laughed. "Even more significant than Jeremy Bentham?"

Bentham had been sitting for a century and a half in a glass case in the corridor of the college.

"Jeremy is the wax figure of a vain philosopher. You are for ever alive, like your alter-ego in the Uffizi. You are the Madonna adoring her holy child, painted by Correggio. The model was his own *inamorata*, later his wife." I took a deep breath: "And you are going to be my wife."

"Me? Yours? How can you say that after an acquaintance-ship of five minutes?"

"Because I love you. Because I've been looking for you all my life."

"All your life? You can hardly be older than me."

"I am twenty. You are eighteen or so, I suspect."

She nodded. "But I can hardly credit a love that fast. Impetuosity. A rush of fleeting emotion."

"You'll see. Don't you feel the electricity in the air? It is sparks created between us."

I took her out next day. We went to a pizzeria in Soho.

(What I described above was true, conversations and all. The truth, but not the whole truth. I described that I was in love with her, *suggesting:* at first sight. Yet it was the manieth sights. I had first noticed her one day in the forecourt, crouching and feeding the sparrows. This act was repeated at several lunch hours. Apparently she hardly went to the refectory, but brought sandwiches from home, some of which were given to the birds. I heard her telephoning her mother once from the public phone of Slade's corridor. She mixed Slavonic words into her fluent English. Also, the occasional Italian expression left her lips too. Painting is a messy job, yet I never saw her hands covered with paint for more than a fleeting minute. She ran to the washroom and returned with clean hands. She had a comb with three pearls, which from time to time adorned her hair. And she had an unmistakable soprano voice: high registers with staccatos and slower, lower, sadder extensions. I was looking for the opportunity when "suavely" I could approach her. Before opening my mouth I looked at her manicured toes in her open-toed sandals. The second was a shade longer than the first, just like those of Signorina Vespucci in Botticelli's painting of the *Birth of Venus*.)

The day following, Sunday, we spent many hours in the National Gallery. Standing in front of *The Sunset* (*Il Tramonto*) by Giorgione; I said it was painted by Zorzo Barbarella. The same name as mine. But, "Your family name is Barbatella. Was it his, as well? Was it not Barbarella?"

"It was. Some people called him Giorgio da Castelfranco. Have you read *Art and Illusion* by Ernst Gombrich?"

"Not yet. May I remind you that I am only a first year student?"

I told Helena that when I was a first year and Professor Ernst discovered me and my name, he said to me: "Young man, quasi Giorgione, you mustn't just draw things and persons to arrange them afterwards in space, but you will really have to think of nature—the earth, the trees, the light, the air, and the clouds, and the human beings with their cities and bridges—as one. Painting with you must now be more than drawing, colouring. It is an art with its own secret laws and devices."

"But sir! I am just Giorgio and not Giorgione," I had said.

"And I," said Helena, "am just drawing and colouring. What have you to do with the Castelfranco family?"

"Well. Dad, who was born in Castelfranco and speaks the Veneto dialect—when he wants—he often calls me Zorzo. The connection is spurious."

"Can I call you Zorzi?" she asked.

I embraced her and kissed her closed mouth.

"Zorzi, you are too brave. *Molto coraggioso*. Kissing me in a picture gallery, in front of so many people . . ."

"That doesn't matter. Those that matter are the tiny figures in *Il Tramonto*. San Rocco, his assistant San Antonio, and San Giorgio, mounted on a rearing horse. The picture in front of you."

"Poor dragon. Aren't you sorry for the creature?"

"No, I'm not because he had incarcerated a young maiden, like you, and wanted to devour her."

At our next meeting—after her first year exams and my finals—I took her to a Czech restaurant in Piccadilly. The meal was good—hunter's steak with dumplings—yet expensive; the music was traditional, we could walk, and dance quick step, and tango.

Helena lived in Wimbledon. When I took her home it was late. Her mother, a thin lady with a chignon, came to open the door and gently admonished her daughter.

"It was my fault," I said. "Please forgive us."

"Well, next time come earlier, and then I'll invite you in. Good-bye, young man . . . ehm. May I know your name?"

This surprised me. Surely, Helena must have told her my name. "I am Giorgio . . . or George, whichever you prefer."

"See you again."

It took some time for me to realise that Helena tended to imprison those facts and events which had touched her sentiments.

She spent the summer in Genoa, staying with her aunt, a fairly well-known violinist. Aunt Jana—whom I was going to meet the following year—had a tiny flat (not more than a cabin) in Sestri Levante, so the two women usually spent weeks at that civilised and historical seaside. Once Byron went there to sail and compose verse, as did Shelley, and perhaps Keats too. Amedeo Grappa painted a whole series of watercolours of the bay.

I corresponded with Helena. My letters were long and enthusiastic, talking about our future and her talent as a painter. Her replies were short but fonder.

Letter, dated 17 August 1986. "*Helena, my love. Congratulations on your birthday on the 20th August. Please add another candle to the nineteen provided by your aunt Jana, for your chocolate cake. That extra candle will burn for our love. Do not blow it out, with the others; let it burn down to the stub into the cake.*

A piece of good news. I am going for an interview at the Chelsea Grammar School (CGS for short). They are looking for a young and energetic art master, to teach first to third year students. It is a mixed school, with internal and external pupils, situated near the Thames and not far from the park where they hold the May flower show.

*I hope you are eating well. When you left in June
you did not have an ounce of extra flesh on you. Not
even on your shapely backside. It is comely to have a
flat tummy but not the ribs which were sticking out at
your side when I embraced you. Allow me to be so bold
as to talk about these relatively intimate parts of yours.*

Tell me about your soggiorno *in Sestri, the taste
of the sea, the walks you had daily, and the new little
pictures you have painted. Which dresses were you
wearing? How about my favourite, the pink mini with
the white dots? I am longing to hold you in my arms,
and kiss your eyes, caress your face, and all the other
parts which your frock protects from my searching
hands.*

With all my love,
Giorgio (Niccolò)"

Her reply came soon: "*Zorzi! Una carezza, H.*"

Yes, I was trying, bodily, physically, to get nearer to my
sweetheart who had been resisting my closer advances vigorous-
ly. "I am a Catholic girl," she said when defending herself
against my bolder moves. "I am a virgin," she said when my
hands were trying to explore territories protected by chemise,
pants and bra, whose colour and texture I was to know by heart.

"There was once a monk, in a monastery where I stayed
overnight, who attempted to make improper advances," she said
once.

"And what happened?"

"I shrieked, as loudly as I could. He retreated. Then I bolt-
ed my door. But sleep eluded me for a while."

"I am not attacking you, ever. I love you."

"I love you too. If you love me, you wait."

"Wait for what? And for how long?"

"To get a job, both of us, to settle down in London properly, and to have the Church bless our union."

"Holy Matrimony? Celebrated, perhaps, by an unholy priest."

"Not out of the question. I mean not all priests are wicked."

This conversation took place after her return to London and was sealed with a passionate kiss. The vision of marriage loomed large.

I did not get the teaching post in Chelsea. I painted: walls, of another school. At Christmas I introduced Helena to Mother and Father. Father kissed her hand, Mother embraced her, and asked directly, "Do you love my son?"

She nodded and embraced Mother again.

I kept applying for other teaching posts. I had an offer in Wandsworth to work as a supply teacher substituting for a woman on pregnancy leave. She was out for a year.

Helena came on Sundays for lunch, right after Church, to our house. One Sunday her mother came too. She talked of her late husband, a ministry official in Prague who had died in mysterious circumstances in the Prague Spring of 1968. He was an enthusiastic follower of Dubček and his policies. His department staged a strike when the Russian tanks came in. Dubček was soon nullified, his team dispersed, his policies shattered. Pavel Hrabikov developed a stomach complaint, and after three days he was dead. There was no autopsy, only a funeral. By that time Zia Jana was a fairly famous violinist with good diplomatic connections. Maria, Helena's mum, made a marriage of convenience with a minor Italian diplomat, which lifted her and her daughter out of Czechoslovakia and landed her in Italy. After that the divorce was immediate. Helena grew up without a father or a substitute father or any male around her. Aunt Jana had a long-time partner, but he was in and out, and was nowhere to be found when she came to London to give a solo concert in the Wigmore Hall, and to see her sister Maria and her niece Helena.

Francesca served polenta with ragout, an unusual combination, followed by zabaglione and champagne grapes. We drank two bottles of Maccarese—a wonderful light white wine which travels badly, but Giuseppe della Croce had brought a caseful as a present hidden among the helmets and sabres and other fencing equipment. During the lunch Helena was more animated than ever before, and I noted that she drank two glasses of wine zestfully. We agreed on a joint family trip to Oxford during her Christmas vacation.

On St Stephen's day, Giorgio, my dad, Helena, Maria and I got into my father's van—Mother felt unwell that day—and drove to Oxford. We got a B & B on Banbury Road and wanted to explore the city, but Helena stopped at St John's College and made a general sketch of it, then used watercolour alfresco. I stayed and watched her. Her mother and my dad went around the centre, and we all met up at George's Hotel for a sandwich lunch and a glass of wine.

The afternoon was spent similarly. Helena stood on Magdalene Bridge and drew, then coloured, the Cherwell Stream running along the garden of the college. I sat next to her on a garden stool reading a book on my namesake Giorgione.

St George's name day is on 24 April. I waited at the Slade school entrance for Helena to finish her day's work. She came out with a friend, a comely Ukrainian girl called Tatyana, and the two of them were shepherded by the portly figure of

Professor Ernst Gombrich, the author of *Art and Illusion,* one of the most profound books (am I able to judge?) of the twentieth century. He greeted me, his one-time student, with a funny salute, touching his left breast (his heart) with his right thumb, then walked away, slightly swaying like a ship on a billowing sea. Tanya stepped up to me, stretched her slim, elegant but paint-covered hand and introduced herself: "I am Tanya, Helena's best friend. You must be the famous Giorgio."

"Giorgio I am, but neither famous, nor infamous."

Helena intercepted further interlocution: "Tanyushka, Giorgio and I are going to celebrate together, tête-à-tête."

"I see. I should be camphor and vanish into thin air. Shouldn't I?"

We did not protest. She walked away pacily, swinging her oversized leather bag, slipping out of the main gate like a schoolgirl trying out hop-skip-and-jump.

Helena and her mother lived in a second-floor flat which looked out on to Wimbledon Common. "When I wake up early," Helena said, "I look out on to the common, and far far away, I spot a womble or two frolicking."

"What colour are they?"

"I cannot be sure. They come out of their burrows shortly before sunrise, when everything is still grey, and disappear back into their holes and tunnels after sunset."

The flat was smallish, but well furnished, comfortable. It had two bedrooms and a living room with an ottoman and three armchairs covered in light leather. Helena's room was white, with white curtains, a white dressing table, a built-in white wardrobe, a bed with white cover, a tiny easel—painted white— and an off-white chest of drawers. The white walls were decorated by the large-postcard size watercolours: stuck on. There were representations of London and Genoa scenes, some alfresco efforts of seaside, lakeside, riverside pictures, two *veduta* of Rome (St Peter's and the Colosseum), where Helena had never been, and three pictures of the Grand Canal in Venice, where she had never been either. The technique was always the same: no attempt was made to create form out of colour—each showed the preparatory drawing on paper. The medium was always paper, very good quality, embossed, bought in large sheets from Antonelli's artist shop in Geneva, then cut to size by the artist. And one more thing: each little town or landscape had one or more tiny figures, and one of these figures seemed to be dancing. Either a female leg was lifted high, or the person tiptoed or she pirouetted, her skirt swirling around her.

A curious feature in the neat room was a pile of refuse in a corner: pencil stubs, worn paintbrushes, *pentimento* fragments and bits and pieces of chewing gum all in a disorderly heap.

"I'll buy you a rubbish bin," said I.

"You shouldn't. Do not try to influence me. Leave me to my little ways."

Aunt Jana came that summer. She let her grey hair down and sailed with us at Swanege in a small pool dinghy which I owned, then swam with Helenka in the lucid sea, and cooked dinner for us all in the cottage we had rented for a weekend. I am a good swimmer, so I was doing a good deal of scuba diving, there and then, and speared some fish. I somehow found myself in a shoal of sea bream, where it was easier to stab one of them than to miss it.

Not long before her finals, Helenka lost her portfolio which contained her drawings, paintings, sketches and written essay for her final exam. After two days of futile search at their flat, in our house, in the tube, on the buses, in the lost property offices, she broke down and cried inconsolably. I'd been trying to console her—in vain. She locked herself in her room for two whole days and nights, without food and drink. They lived on the second floor. I climbed up the drainpipe, broke a window-pane and took a thermos of cocoa to her. She drank it, then climbed back into bed where she had been. A day later Maria packed Helena's bag, bought her a ticket, and sent her to Jana in Genoa to recover.

While the two of them were at London airport, I took off the large-postcard size aquarelles from the walls of her room, put them in my portfolio and carried the lot to the Slade school at University College. I spoke to Ernst Gombrich, Rudolf Wittcover, a certain Professor Jones, the chairman of the examinations board, and told them the story of Helena's lost portfolio and of the owner's distress.

They hummed and hawed and referred the matter to yet another board, which—eventually—came to the conclusion that Helena Hrabikova was to be awarded a diploma. When Maria and I heard that, we phoned Jana and Helena, and the latter returned, thinner than ever, but happy.

Soon after that I got a permanent teaching post in Fulham High School—where boys and girls studied or wasted their time—and she got a job as a picture restorer's assistant in Kensington High Street. At Christmas we got married in Brompton Oratory. The wedding was a modest affair, yet, sur-prisingly, almost all our close relatives were there: her mother and her aunt, my parents, my dad's sister Giuliana, her husband Benedetto, Lucia from Castelfranco and Giuseppe della Croce. It was Giuseppe who had brokered the family truce, perhaps not so surprising after so many years in the wilderness of unfriend-liness.

Lucia was petite, with ash blonde hair and a hardly noticeable limp. Benedetto was muscular—he used to be not just a gondolier but a one-time wrestler—with kohlrabi ears. Aunt Giuliana was still a beauty.

And there was one surprise member—not ever seen by me before—a certain Jirar Azirjan, Jana's friend, a well-to-do antiquarian of Milan. Azirjan was a small man with greying black hair and bushy knitted eyebrows. He had a long, narrow head, an interminable rocky-boned forehead and chin, a big shapeless nose and two black eyes darting to and fro.

Helena and I spent the wedding night in my room in Fulham, then took off by an Alitalia jet to Venice, where we were booked into an elegant hotel on the Grand Canal, called Principe. The owner was a portly Austrian, with a handsome priest of a son called Karl. Our room had a balcony, with two easy chairs, looking out on to the Grand Canal.

Helena was happy, I was gentle, the *Tramontana* wind was moderate in strength, the place was devoid of tourists, the ringing of the midday bells of St Mark's and of the two Moors resounded in the cool air. We walked up the stairs, I placed Helena between the two bronze bell ringers and made a snapshot of the three of them with the Doge's Palace in the background. In the afternoon we crossed the Rialto, or rather I crossed it. Helena fell and sprained her left ankle. Her otherwise pinched, trim ankle swelled up to large cucumber size, my newly-wed wife cried like a babe, and I had to carry her—in several *étapes*—back to the hotel.

"*Veni, vidi sed non vici,*" she said, sitting on the balcony, left food bandaged and iced, and supported on a *predella*, a small prayer stool provided by the priest. She spent the week in that way, pad on her leg, drawing and painting vaporettos, gondolas, palaces with loggias and the waves of the water. She was not unhappy. Little dancing figures (sometimes a woman, sometimes a man) still appeared on her aquarelles. And she discovered something I had missed. Two divers were submerging and re-emerging in the water amongst the pillars of the *palazzo* opposite. They were examining the damage caused by centuries of salty water on the poles. "Venice will be totally covered by the sea," said my wife, and tears glistened in her eyes.

I was her servant, fetching orange juice from the pack, helping her to the toilet then to the dining table. I snatched some time between meals to visit the Accademia and see Giorgione's two best pictures there. Of course, I had known them from reproductions, even read about them previously, but the impact of seeing the real thing was immediate and has stayed with me ever since. *La Vecchia* is a relatively small portrait of an old yet still active woman. Painted on canvas and practically square, it shows a woman in her sixties with a small kerchief covering her hair, dressed modestly in countrywomen's style, in white and light-red garb, showing healthy teeth and active hands.

Compare the old lady's lower lip and nose to those of Giorgione in the self-portrait of the painter kept in the Szépmüvészeti Múzeum, Budapest. One can discover similarities—not decisive, but likely ones. I had a feeling, but no proof, that she might have been the painter's mother. If so, and if painted in 1500, her painter son must have been twenty-six years old at the time. Whereas the guides speak of such influences as Leonardo or even Dürer—both of whom had visited Venice and might have met Giorgione—still I think it is not necessary to seek outside influences when painting a realistic portrait.

Giorgione was, as attested by a range of his paintings, capable of *sfumato*, preferred, wherever, whenever appropriate, placing his subjects in a landscape, as part of the landscape; blurring some of the contours in order to increase the atmosphere and mystery, and using many colours to suggest the feel and the mood of nature. I spent half a day with *La Vecchia*, then returned to the Principe.

"No birds!" exclaimed Helena, as soon as I appeared.

"There are some gulls."

"Not many. And then nothing else."

"It is winter, January."

"Still. Where are the sparrows?"

"Dearest, as soon as you can walk we will visit St Mark's square and the multitude of pigeons there."

3. Tracking Giorgione

"He fell so deeply in love with the beauties of nature that he would represent his work only when he copied directly from life."

(Vasari)

The next day Helena was better. She borrowed crutches, hobbled down the steps, and we had lunch at a nearby restaurant. Then we took the *vaporetto* to the Accademia. No drawing pad with her, just a camera hanging down from her left shoulder which she had hoped to use, but wasn't allowed to by the attendant. Although she did not share my enthusiasm for Giorgione—a painter who was reputed to omit preparatory drawing for his figures in paint—she shared my curiosity.

"So small," she breathed, standing in front of *The Tempest*. "Just about bigger than the biggest Salvador Dalí."

"It is not the size that counts," I quaked. "He conjured in that oblong of a canvas 800 by 700 mm more wonders than other painters put in a whole gallery."

"Granted. But I am a bit tired."

For a small tip I borrowed the chair of the large-moustached attendant, and Helena sat down.

"What is he telling us with this picture? Is it a pastoral scene with a shepherd, and his girlfriend, suckling a baby, alfresco, just about the wrong time when the tempest is about to break out?" Helena asked.

"Things in nature may not have happened the way they were painted. Pictures have a pre-birth. They are begotten in the mind; they have a pre-birth in the eyes, in the images you see, in your dreams. The hands are obedient servants only," I said.

"It may be so. The shepherd could be a soldier, the nude mother might be a gypsy—while on the other hand the baby might just be the infant Paris."

"If so, the soldier is no soldier, the stark naked woman no gypsy, and the storm no accident—the whole scene was conceived by Zeus."

"Not quite starkers, is she? Observe the sheet under her bum and the shoulder piece. The bridge over the stream is not Hellenistic; the buildings beyond are positively fifteenth- to eighteenth-century Italian edifices. Yet, with a little far-fetched imagination we could conjecture that the twin towers in the picture might represent the tombs of Paris and Oenone," Helena suggested.

"And the tempest above might not be coming; it might be going. The trees and bushes of the picture, either above the figures or beyond them, are not moved by the wind, which should be part and parcel of a storm. There is only one patch of rain."

"Neither is the water turbulent in the stream," she argued.

"You know what our master, the wizard Gombrich, said?"

"I suppose, that the picture represents matters in a becalmed afternoon rather than in a fresh morning."

"Giorgione has not drawn objects and people to arrange them afterwards in space, but he really thought of nature, the earth, the trees, the light, air and clouds, and the human beings with their cities and bridges as one. In a way, this was almost as big a step forward into a new realm as the discovery of perspective had been. From now on, painting was more than drawing plus colouring. It was an art with its own secret laws and devices."

"Nonetheless, whatever is achieved was done with paint. I envy his variety of greens. The dominant is, I think, copper green in the vegetation. Perhaps it was mixed with copper resinate, lead white, some yellow, and red ochres with burnt umber."

"I'll tell you something. The pundits have been guessing who she might be, might have been—I mean who the model was. No clues. But just compare the frontal view of Judith. Her left foot—in the Hermitage picture—is placed on the head of Holofernes. It is the same (or very similar) female foot the lady of the *Passing Storm* (for this is what I would call the painting) displays. Judith's left leg is uncovered to the thigh, and it could be identical to the left leg in the sitting position of the lady looking at us under the bushes."

"It is a conjecture which cannot either be proved or denied," said Helena. "And, indeed, the hair colour of the two ladies is identical, and the hair styles aren't much different. But the mother's figure is well padded while Judith is much slimmer."

"Well, Judith has small, girlish, sensitive breasts like someone I know."

"Go away. Next you'll say that I was his model."

"No, I wouldn't. *Judith* was painted in 1504 and the *Passing Storm* in 1510. The model could have been the same lady—perhaps a favourite girlfriend of Giorgione's—who filled out after childbirth. But no, the two faces are different."

"For that matter have a look at the lad, at the left hand front corner of the picture. Who's he?" she asked.

"Soldier, shepherd, mythological figure, fellow from Zorzo's imagination, guard, the dad of the suckling babe, a *ragazzo* too well dressed for the *campagna* . . ."

"Yes, that's it," Helena said. "Too well dressed in a silk shirt, red doublet, fancy breeches and stockings of fashionably unmatching colours. He is looking at his lady-ward with a protective turn of his head, and his right hand is lightly holding his long stick."

"The rod has no metal head, so it is not the shaft of a lance, nor is it a crooked shepherd's stick. It could be the seven foot standard measuring rod used by painters at preparing frescoes. Another giveaway is hair, this splendid head of hair, the *zazzera,* almost the same in colour and shape as Giorgione's own on his self-portrait, kept in Budapest," I noted.

"So could it be a Giorgione self-portrait?"

"What I think is this: the model for the young man was Giorgione himself, the model for the young mother was his girl-friend. We have no record of Zorzo having had a son, but he could have had one."

"It is quite certain, isn't it, that the child is a boy?"

"Unmistakably. Some owners in the nineteenth century referred to the painting as the family of Giorgione: *the painter, his lover Cecilia, and their son.* The figures do not appear to represent themselves, a sixteenth-century painter and his lass, they represent mythological figures. Paris is not the child but the father, the very same standing young man. The woman is his wife, called Oenone, a daughter of the Ilian river Kebren. The son is called Corythos."

"Giorgio, have you spotted that white bird on the roof top of the first building?"

"I have. It is a white heron. I would say a dwarf heron. It occurs in Virgil's *Georgica . . . ardea significant tempestatem.*"

"What about the *pentimentos?* Weren't there any?"

The drumming of a sudden shower on the roof and on the

windowpanes swept my answer away. It was not a tempest insofar as the sky outside lacked lightning within our vision, and the oncoming rain of cats and dogs lacked the deep rumble of the dark clouds. The building was waterproof, yet every visitor seemed to congregate in one corner where a small bar offered beverages and *elemosina* to people in the queue and to the non-queuing attendants of the Accademia. We had a *capuccino* each, talked to a middle-aged fat lady wearing an enormous felt hat, then returned to our painting.

Helena, once again seated, said: "There is an unequal spreading of paint: the lad and his foreground have more of it than the poplars beyond the bridge . . . and the eucalyptus least of all."

"Wait a minute, Fawn." (This was one of my pet names for her.) "A recent examination of the picture revealed two *pentimentos*. There had been a tree or two instead of the twin towers in the background, and the lad—as you call him—in front seemed to have changed places with his lady friend."

"The other thing I miss in the picture is the contours. Botticelli, who after all was a Florentine, an older contemporary of Giorgione's—although they may not have known each other—painted, or drew and painted, very sharp divisions in his pictures between each human figure or, for that matter, between each piece of the flora and the fauna. Recall his flower petals, and butterflies in *Primavera*; visualise the profiles of Venus, and Mars on his elongated quadro."

"Well, take Leonardo. He uses *sfumato* even more profusely than Giorgione. The clarity of air in Florence—an inland city—may be contrasted to the light mist of the northern Italian, and particularly the Venetian air. Tall George may or may not have used a pencil or a chalk to sketch his figures, and for landscapes he may have only used his brush and paints."

"Like Renoir in the nineteenth century."

"The rain has stopped; let's go home to Hotel Principe."

I took no risk and carried my wife and her crutches straight into the *vaporetto*.

Surprise in the foyer of the hotel. Under a gilded branch—I could not decide whether real or waxwork—two smallish figures were sipping their Campari's: Helena's aunt Jana and Jirar Azirjan, her Armenian antiquarian companion. Jana wore a light yellow dress with a red speck under the neck where the Campari had left its mark; Jirar had a white suit on with a lilac tie and a blue rose in his lapel. His spats were slightly speckled. He was cleaning them with his white handkerchief. "The rain," he said, "the rain."

The two women embraced and kissed each other. Jana began to caress Helena's face uttering endearing Slavonic words I could not understand.

I ordered a Campari too, and as it landed on the gilded lion-feet table, a late fly dived into it. It swam around helplessly, and I neither assisted nor killed it. Then it found the straw and climbed out, like a drowning shipwreck victim escaping to a plank of wood.

Jirar, who must have been noticing the fly's struggle, spoke up: "Giorgio, there is a silver cup by Cellini, at least I think it is, which features a wasp, or a bee (I'm not sure which) climbing out of the vessel and grabbing the edge with his first two feet. It is made of gold, 18 carats."

"There are relatively few works of Cellini that survived the sack of Rome, the centuries and the collectors' greed," I pondered.

"Have you heard of the Del Pieros of Milan?"

At that time the famous soccer star might just have been a small boy, so at that time I knew of no Del Pieros.

Jirar took out a coloured photo from his shirt wallet. The silver cup had a ring of semiprecious stones around it, and at its base displayed the Del Pieros' crest, a crab holding a brooch with the date MLXXVIII.

"So far so good. But how can you say that this cup with the *wasp*—it is a *wasp!*—is the creation of that genius of a black-guard Benvenuto Cellini?"

"Well, if you keep on handling and twisting, tumbling the tumbler, you will still find no sign that proves, or hints, that it is the work of Cellini. At the most: it is the workmanship; we can almost hear the wasp buzzing. But there is something else: the diary of Vincenzo Del Piero from the 1520s. We find an entry, January 1525, which says: "ordered a chalice from Benvenuto". And then, three years later, another: "My love Clara (his wife) rejoices when drinking from the Benvenuto chalice.""

I thought that there were more Benvenutos than Cellini Benvenutos in the 1520s in Italy, but said nothing.

We all went to have supper at the Rialto restaurant, at the foot of the bridge. Jirar ordered a fourteen-ounce lobster (in honour of the Del Pieros' crest), Helena and I ate black caviar—knowing its anecdotal amorous quality— and Jana ate calamari with brown rice.

The restaurant had atmospheric light with lanterns hanging down from the ceiling and large candles illuminating the tables. Ours had two visitors: a late butterfly and an early moth circled around the flame.

We polished off a bottle of sweet Italian champagne, omit-ted the *Segafredo*, and finished with Strega *bolla*. Jirar paid the bill. He proposed a toast to our marriage. Jana and Jirar were staying in the Principe. It was Helena who had contacted her aunt—after the accident—but it was Jirar who had proposed that they come and who had driven in his Merc.

Breakfast was breezy on the terrace looking out to the Grand Canal. The night had passed with two libations to Venus. Helena ate a double breakfast: two croissants and a jellied eel. I followed suit with kippers, a pint of orange juice and stewed fruit. Jirar proposed a tour in a gondola, but Helena felt awkward and tired, and wanted to continue *chiachierare* (to chat) with her aunt. Jirar and I walked to the Hall of the Great Council in the Doge's Palace to see Tintoretto's *Paradise* there, and leaving the hotel we heard the ethereal sound of Jana's violin; she was playing the chords of a Mozart sonata.

Jirar remarked: "Bernini was, I suppose, Bach, in terms of music; Beethoven was surely Michelangelo; Mozart was the musical rebirth of Raffaello. But who was Giorgione?"

"Either Purcell or Monteverdi."

The sun's fire was reduced by nimble breezes blowing from the sea creating a kind of draft on the *piazza* in front of the Basilica of St Mark and somehow entering the Doge's Palace— if ever so faintly.

"Is there a painting anywhere bigger than this Tintoretto?" asked Jirar. "I mean painting, not fresco?"

"I don't know for sure. Perhaps a Tiepolo."

"They say Tintoretto had won a competition, unfairly, to paint this *Paradise* with Christ, the Virgin Mary, the angels and the saints."

"Yes. He broke into the chamber, smuggled in a painting of his, and before you could say Jack Robinson or Robinson Crusoe . . ."

"He got the commission to paint *Paradise*."

"At any rate, the Council used the Venetian painter of his time, who registered a cavalcade of bodies—some with well-known Venetian faces—up on the wall."

"And what about your hobby horse, Giorgione? Few bodies, much landscape, eh?"

"He painted little and died early. Wine, women and song were as important for him as painting. His lute was as dear to him as his brush. His friend Titian not only outlived him by decades but had attained his technique, finished some of his pictures and flooded his growing clientele with masterworks."

"Should a Titian picture and a Giorgione painting come on the market—say two canvasses roughly the same size—which would fetch a higher price at an auction in London?" asked Jirar.

"Hmm. I think da Castelfranco, because of its rarity value. We know only seventeen paintings authentically attributed to him without qualms of the *cognoscenti*, whereas there are hundreds of Titians."

"While Titian was mixing red madder
His model was crouched on a ladder
Her position to Titian
Suggested coition
So he stopped mixing madder and had her."

Jirar laughed, holding his shaking paunch. Then he said, "What if we found another Giorgione, I mean not just one, but many, bound in a book, all extremely small but undoubtedly genuine?"

I looked at him with widely opened eyes. "This is totally unlikely. The master died in 1510 when printing was still in its infancy. Who would have asked Zorzo to illustrate a book?"

We walked into Danieli's, where the food is tops, and the people are as rich as the tips Jirar gave to the headwaiter. He ordered clams and champagne, coffee ice-cream and Irish coffee. We ate moderately.

Jirar lit a cigar and comfortably, luxuriously puffed out concentric circles of scented smoke. "It was a book of hours, a kind of prayer book which used to belong to the Marchioness of Mantua, Isabella d'Este. Her land was not a papal but an imperial *feudum*. Gonzaga got his title from Sigismund, Holy Roman emperor and Hungarian king."

I pricked up my ears like a beagle scenting a hare.

"We know that in October 1510 the Marchese wrote to her agent in Venice asking him to acquire a night scene, *una nocte*, by Giorgione," I said.

"I know about that. The master, his illness unknown to anyone at the time, was to die within a month," replied Jirar.

"He did die, before 8 November 1510, as attested by Taddeo Albano replying to Isabella d'Este. '*A che rispondo a V. Ex che ditto Zorzo morí piu di fanno da peste.*'" ("I am responding to your Excellency's [letter] that the same Zorzo [Giorgione] has died of the plague.")

The plague in Veneto—including Venice itself—was one of the worst in the region during the returning waves of pestilence in the sixteenth century. Almost always the pandemic arrived, surreptitiously, on ships hailing from the East, and almost always the only "remedy" was quick-lime or slaked-lime. When chlorine was discovered and used, it proved to be more effective.

The carriers of the plague were initially rat fleas, but eventually humans too. It spread by infected droplets expelled during coughing. There is an unauthenticated story that Giorgione caught it from his lover, Cecilia, who had summoned him to her bedside.

"The dating of Taddeo Albano's letter ties in with my suspicions. We have to see the *Book of Hours*. Where is it?"

"I have a photo of its first page in my flat in Milan. Its owner—a minor member of the Este family—was contemplating letting Sotheby's auction it, sometime next year. So they too have a coloured photo of page one—or sheet one, as you might call it. I understand that their agent visited Ferrara and made copious notes of the book."

"And how do you come in if, in fact, Sotheby's already have a hand on it?"

"This way. If and when the book is auctioned, I will bid for it as commissioned by my client."

"And who might that be . . . may I know?"

"Only if you swear to secrecy."

"I swear on the Bible." As in every good hotel room, even ours at the Principe, where we were to return later, there was a copy of the Bible. I would solemnly swear on it.

"*Bene*. The Library of Congress in Washington is my client. The director has given me the mandate."

Next morning Jirar Azirjan and Jana Blindalova left Venice for Milan.

It was a glorious early summer's day. Helena wore a long white dress, reaching down to her ankles, with large sunflowers, whose originals had once been designed by Van Gogh. She cast away her crutches, like the cripple whom Jesus had cured, and went down the stairs, step by step, carefully entering the gondola called up late that afternoon. I wore a pair of grey flannel trousers and a white shirt, brown sandals, no socks. The gondolier—at the middle of his middle years—wore the "uniform": straw hat, striped shirt, dark blue trousers and soft black shoes. He stood on a Turkish carpet at the back of his boat, facing us, as we were looking at the *immediate port,* the canalscape of our journey. (This was the first and last journey I took in a gondola—although years later I frequented a London pub called The Gondola.)

Now we started on the Grand Canal, with the setting sun behind us, and finished, maybe two hours later—having done a round voyage—with the rising moon in front of us.

Helena had once before been to Venice, with her mother, Maria, so she whooped with joy as she recounted to me the sights of the Fondaco dei Turchi, the *Ca' Pesaro,* the Ca' d'Oro and the Fondaco dei Tedeschi, rebuilt.

"I would have loved to have seen the original building," I remarked.

"Why, isn't this the original?"

"Not quite. The original was painted, decorated, frescoed by Giorgione and his helpers. But it caught fire . . . just as the one before that had done. La Fenice, the opera house, was also burnt down but then rebuilt four times.

"And you, don't you catch fire?" The great brown eyes hooked their rays into my dark eyes. She inched nearer on the bench, and I felt her thighs as hot as a warming furnace.

I called out to the gondolier: "Fasten the fabric of the canopy, keep on rowing, and don't disturb us until I call for you."

"*Sissignore. Ma posso cantare?*" ("Yessir. May I sing?")

"Sing away."

I moved back with Helena to the generous davenport.

She took both my hands. "Do you love me?"

"Of course I do. You know that. Ever since I set eyes on you."

"I remember that, but I don't know *how much* you love me."

"I love you very much."

"But is that enough? Are you *madly* in love with me?"

I didn't know what to say. Madness had never entered my mind in connection with our relationship. Protection, yes. Tenderness, yes. Uncritical devotion, yes. Occasional adoration, yes. Physical desire, yes. Through a slit in the fabric of the canopy above me, I spotted the half moon wandering amongst floating clouds, like a widow looking for the grave of her husband in a cemetery.

"Giorgio. You are silent? Are you madly in love with me— or are you not?"

"Helena, the concept of madness is alien to me."

"But not to me. Inside the complex interior, madness lurks in me. Sometimes I find it hard to suppress it. Beware. If it breaks out one day, you will only be able to cope with it if you possess at least a modicum of madness in your love."

She began to unbutton the large round buttons on her sunflower dress. She had never before initiated love making. We lay down, magnet and iron. The silky core of the divan brought new sensations to our bare skins. My body infused the valley between her long, girlish thighs. She (as she told me later) felt a thirst, and hunger that she had not known before, but not for food or drink. (Sexual desire, like hunger, is regulated by a centre that stimulates sensitivity to dopamine and depresses sensitivity to seratonin. In the course of sexual excitement blood vessels expand, and this is brought about by the parasympathetic nerves. The clitoris swells and the little veins around the vagina expand, while its interior becomes more slippery under the influence of oestrogen.)

The goddess Tosi stands over lovers; when the dam is opened the stream of life makes its way towards its happy goal.

The clitoris stiffens and the vagina, rich in nerve-endings, plays like a bow on a string on the male instrument that releases the sperm, targeted like rockets on the shining star of the seed within the ovum.

4. Book of Hours

*"Prayers may not often be answered
but they maintain equilibrium."*

(Huizinga)

While drawing, and painting, teaching the basics to my art classes about the craft, and the art forms relating to sundry materials, I kept on reawakening to two things, one plus, one minus. I did like and I do like teaching: seeing a rough diamond perfected, a budding talent grow wings. I understand and explain techniques well, including the ancient ones of tempera or using a blank wall for murals or selecting and preparing wood panels instead of canvas. And I acquaint them even with the new improved technique of xerography. I can explain and demonstrate the art of sculpting, but I have never created an outstanding painting or a fully competent drawing or a truly expressive piece of sculpture.

Helena, on the other hand, had real talent. Her aquarelles were telling pictures, speaking of a pair of eyes able to perceive impressionistically a slice of reality within a given vista, a seascape, landscape or townscape, and fill it with sentiment. There were little people in them. And her pictures exuded freshness. The dancing girl was always there, the sun—sometimes half hidden—was mostly shining, sometimes faintly, sometimes with full force, and there was a breeze, visible by the moving foliage, ever present in her paintings.

Happy canvasses. We were not badly off, so she needed no regular weekday work. Some of her pictures found outlets in Italy through the connections of Jirar Azirjan, others were sold at Harrods where she had a corner for a tiny permanent exhibition in the furniture department. The manager of the department was the father of Helena's friend Tatyana, a budding sculptor herself.

Perhaps it was significant, perhaps not, that a boy of sixteen, called Mike Blood, drew a caricature portrait of me during an art class, when he should have been drawing a vase. He did draw the vase—an imitation of a Hellenistic vessel—with my face on it and two large ears hanging down from it, either side, left and right.

"Why?" I asked him indignantly, but without anger.

"Long ears mean wisdom," said Mike Blood.

That wisdom has led me to seek other outlets (or a different route for a different talent) of my character. (Or is it *make-up* or is it *personality?*) Fortunately I was not thinking of Michelangelo's revenge on Biago, when he painted him with donkey's ears, nor of the unfortunate Marsyas, nor the long-eared Lapiths.

I kept on trying. I experimented with woodwork and carved little figurines—shepherds of the Veneto region, navvies of the London docks—but all turned out to be awkward amateurish efforts. I tried acrylic paint, which gives quick and early results, but I only managed to cover the canvasses with layers of paint either representing cumbersome, lifeless figures or—when doing an abstract—meaningless blotches. Helena never praised nor criticised my work. She was—has always been—wrapped up in her own creative work.

One day, taking Helena's new large postcard pictures to Tatyana's father, Mr Corwen in Harrods, and collecting the takings of the last sale of her pictures there, I blurted out that I had no talent, myself. I showed him some of my paintings with self-disgust. Corwen looked at me hard. He was a dapper figure, a smallish man with longish ears, an angular face and a self-taught and a very elegant accent—suitable for a very elegant clientele. A Ukrainian Jewish emigrant (his original name was Corah), he was a model of assimilation.

"Mr Barbatella, your forte is not *creating* art—which at best (forgive me) could just be mediocre—but *interpreting* it. Great art, the art of masters: deal with them, interpret them."

His opinion had not surprised me. We are, at the least, always hoping for approval for our own thoughts. For confirmation I consulted my former teachers at the Slade. There was a possibility of doing an MA by thesis in the History of Art section so long as one found the right topic, and the right expert teacher to be one's tutor.

At Christmas we were invited to Jana's, not to Via Boccadasse in Genoa, but to the large apartment Jirar owned in Milan. I was particularly looking forward to the trip because it offered a viewing of the photograph of a page of the *Book of Hours* that once had belonged, allegedly, to the Marchioness of Mantua, Isabella d'Este.

Jirar lived on the second floor of a *palazzo* between the Galleria and the Scala. The marble staircase was accentuated at every turn with a red porphyry fawn standing to attention. The doorknob was a white ivory ram's head.

The door, with three separate locks, led straight into the salon, spacious and luxurious. You walked on thick Turkish carpets, woven together, as it were, displaying four *mihrabs*.

The salon had four torch-bearing Moors, whose lights could be dimmed, and one central sparkling Venetian chandelier. One side of the room, including the inner side of the door, was covered with antique books which, when the door was shut, gave a tromp l'oeil effect. There was a seventeenth-century dinner table in the middle of the room, with large drawers holding the silver knives and forks, and a whole service of plates for twelve, although the oak table could not seat more than eight. The chairs were covered with soft cushions of calf leather, each with different decorations of Armenian crests of various regions.

There was a large painting on the wall: *The Resurrection of Lazarus.* This friend of Christ was a favourite subject of art to the Armenians, perhaps because His resurrection reminded them of Armenia's resurrection. The painting, by an unidentified artist of the seventeenth century, showed Lazarus—a handsome young man, with the pale skin of the dead—stretching his right hand towards Christ, standing in blinding glory in front of the cave grave. In the background the two sisters, with gaping mouths, fall on their knees. Next to them, on the ground, a skull and thigh bone. Death and life.

Azirjan had a shop on Via Manzoni, so he did not fill his abode with many antique pieces; there was, however, another smaller painting, this time by Bassano, showing some disciples of Christ having a meal, and a Renaissance stool inlaid with semi-precious stones. All showy pieces, nothing of great value. His desk, ruled by a bronze lion in the middle and displaying twelve drawers, was placed near the large fireplace. There was a purple heart chess table with an inlaid board in front of the fireplace and two Persian cushions, either side.

"Wouldn't you like a game of chess?" asked my host.

I agreed. I was, I am, a mediocre chess player. I was check-mated in twelve moves.

The apartment was air conditioned—but in winter, instead of upping the heating, Azirjan lit the fire for effect, and to boost the temperature. Well, it was lit in truth by his non-speaking relative, an older woman with a chignon, who had her own room and shower at the back of the flat. The Moor standing between the fireplace and the desk held a torch in his right hand, while the lifting of his left hand opened a swing door which swallowed the desk and brought forward a double bed.

"A modern contraption," I said.

"You are mistaken, my friend; this whole set-up was brought here from the castle of Bracciano, where it had been constructed towards the end of the fifteenth century. The Pallavicini-Odeschalchi family had dispersed some of their rich-es, including pieces of the castle's furniture. No one really want-ed it, I got it relatively cheaply."

Helena and I were placed in the bedroom next door, the rooms connected by a long bathroom which was cut into two. Our bedroom was plain, apart from a baroque chest of drawers with a decorated commode and the mattress on the bed, which was made of the same material the moonlanders had used in 1969.

On New Year's Day we, all four of us, went to the midday mass, celebrated by the archbishop in the cathedral. At "*Dona nobis pacem*", Helena suddenly had to go to the toilet. I alerted a verger and he—*ohne genier*—put her into a lift. She could relieve herself at the toilet at the rear of the church, fitted amongst the multitude of small gothic towers. This inspired a significant aquarelle by Helena—extravagantly bigger than all her other paintings. On it we saw one hundred towers, each numbered, and a large Coca-Cola box in between them. The box had the toilet seat, a young woman sitting on it with a growing belly. Helena was pregnant. The picture is private; it is hanging in our bedroom.

In the evening we all went to La Scala where Jirar had been renting box B32. Before that, practically all day long (between the morning mass and the evening concert), Jana was practising at home, then rehearsing at La Scala. Although the variety programme had not really required the presence of a conductor, there was one in the person of Claudio Abbado, friendly, elegant and vocal. The New Year's concert—while it is fully Strauss in Vienna, Dublin or Budapest—was a variety of tasteful dishes in Milan: madrigals, sonatas and organ variations. Three madrigals were sung by Kiri Te Kanawa, the Mozart sonatas were played by Radu Lupu, piano, and Jana Blindalova, violin. The Bach organ variations were played by a Dublin organist, Gerard Gillen, a brilliant understudy to Signor Cavalcanti who had flu at the time. After the concert we had a midnight reception by the *sindaco* mayor; I kissed the right hand of Kiri Te Kanawa, and Jirar Azirjan invited Claudio Abbado to a late breakfast in the Galleria.

Noviter impressis . . . Parisius imprensis . . . Almanach pour XVI, Ans . . . Ianus Februs Martius . . . November Dies XXX. These notes were added to the copy by Jirar Azirjan, who had studied the entire book, with his scratchy, angular handwriting.

The miniature on the given leaf is that of Mary, received by her mother, St Anne, with the figure of an unknown third young woman behind the heavily pregnant Virgin. In the immediate background, the thick foliage of a beech tree frames the picture; on the left hand side of the full leaf (as we were looking at it) there is a blue corner, consisting of the morning sky, a nearby tower and a faraway promontory. There is a group of other buildings on the top of a tallish mountain. Two colours dominate: the blue cloak of the Virgin (aquamarine) and the red dress of her mother (madder). The golden halos (presumably liquidised gold dust) of the two saints are definitive. I would say that the season supported by the picture is spring. But if spring, how come that Mary is heavily pregnant? If Jesus was born at Christmas, then a November landscape would have been more appropriate.

The representation is artistic, not only in the refined faces of a welcoming middle-aged mother and her beautiful young daughter—her face betrays serenity and submission—but because there is a repeated movement of undulation between the figures of the two women. They are holding hands, and the folds of their garbs complement the hands.

I could hardly wait for the time of my Easter vacation, when I would have the chance for a visit to Ferrara.

It also occurred to me that I had seen the reproduction of two paintings in a Hungarian art book claiming that those two exquisite paintings, showing Mary and Anne, were done by a master whose initials only were known—a mysterious M.S.

The Slade was accommodating. I had a topic: *"The Gonzaga Book of Hours"*. Soon I had a tutor in the person of Dr Peter Taylor, curator of the Renaissance holdings in the Courtauld Institute's Gallery, lecturer in History of Art at the Slade, and a very agreeable, bright and nimble gentleman. He was an expert on the *vedute,* the pictures and guidebooks on Rome, composed between 1500–1700.

"I am eager to know about your discovery, Giorgio," said

he. "To supervise you will be a learning curve for me as well as for you." Peter reminded me of a handsome squirrel, who gathers, perhaps, a thousand nuts to be stored for the winter, yet eats only a hundred.

Joy exists, and if repeated in our lives it creates a climate of happiness. But the clear skies are often threatened by dark clouds, so the climate of happiness may change into brooding sadness. Helena had abdominal pains which her doctor, our GP Dr Steele, diagnosed as stomach troubles. The pains were sporadic but increased in intensity. We made an appointment with Alphonse Greene, a renowned gynaecologist. Examination, X-ray, an operation was projected for the next day. It was that urgent. He explained: "Your wife has an ectopic pregnancy. This means that the foetus is outside the womb. This condition is not too rare . . ."

"But can the child be aborted, and kept alive?"

Greene, a large man with large cauliflower ears and massive paws, looked at me and spoke with pity in his voice.

"The embryo is not likely to be alive. If it was in the cervix, it might have had some space for itself, but as it is in the left ovary, it does not. Your wife's condition is life threatening. Was she bleeding at all during the last two months?"

"We have to ask her."

She had not been bleeding at all, which, for her, was a sign of her pregnancy going well.

I sat next to her bed after the operation, waiting for her to wake up from the anaesthetic. When she did I held her hands. Hours passed, and she said nothing. Her face was white as a sheet, and, at one point, her hazel eyes filled with tears. Maria, her mum, happened to be in Genoa with her sister at the time. I rang my parents. Babbo brought a bunch of lilies, Mamma brought a selection of compotes (Helena's favourites)—cherry, pear, mango and peach. She ate nothing, nothing for days. When she came out of hospital, after four days, she was lighter by eight pounds.

I postponed the Ferrara trip and did some homework—with Peter Taylor helping in the background—on Isabella d'Este, Marchioness of Mantua. Her husband seemed to have been a stupid brute. She was born in Ferrara in 1474, the second daughter of the duke, Ercole d'Este, and his wife, Eleonora of Aragon. At the age of sixteen she married Marquis Francesco Gonzaga. We have a portrait painted at the tenth wedding anniversary of Isabella, in 1500, by Titian. This shows a thoughtful young lady, grand in her dress, with keen intelligence radiating from her handsome, cute face. The eyes are set wide, the face is round, the neck has a gentle arch. She wears an ermine coat and a tall, turban-like headdress which allows us to see her bronze hair.

For reasons unknown to me, this three-quarter length painting, which now hangs in the Kunsthistorisches Museum in Vienna, is dated 1536 by Titian experts. In that year Isabella was sixty-two, and was to die three years later. There is another portrait—artist unidentified—which shows her as a middle-aged lady, wearing a dark dress with a white top.

Of her younger brothers: Ippolito was elevated to be a cardinal in early life, and his munificence was responsible for the creation of the Garden of Tivoli with its splendour of palace and fountains. Like all the d'Este, Isabella homed in on collecting art and sponsoring artists.

Her association with Leonardo da Vinci bore fruit in his picture of her, later in life, but the "black and white profile" drawn by him (in fact red chalk and yellow pastel) was an unripe fruit; it remained one of many of Leonardo's unfinished portraits.

Her husband, the marquis, was an unworthy fellow. A serial adulterer, he was the captain of the League against the French intervention. He was captured and kept as a prisoner for many years—until finally he was freed, due to his wife's diplomatic skills, in 1519.

While her husband was in prison, and at various times after that, she carried the load of governing on her shoulders while continuing to collect art objects in the best taste: manuscripts, early printed books (i.e. contemporary printed books), musical instruments—she was an accomplished lutist—maps, bronzes and pictures. The catalogue of her art treasures in her palace ran to 1,600 objects—today we can identify only three pieces.

"Who else among the masters might we associate with Isabella?" I asked Peter Taylor.

"Mantegna, for sure, although they did not really like one another. In 1497 she persuaded him to improve the interior of the ducal apartment. The results were the *studiolo* paintings: two by Mantegna, one by Perugino, two by del Costa, two by Correggio. With this set of pictures we associate the *Hypnerotomachia Poliphili*, a book of a journey of dreams, half real, half allegorical, the most beautifully illustrated book ever produced.

"But even if we can associate it with Isabella or her circle of Ferrara or Mantua, her seat was not far from Venice, where Aldo Manutio printed the book in 1499, nor far from Florence, either, where it had been dreamed up; but the date would be too early with a Giorgione association. He was only twenty-two when the book appeared, and only seventeen when its illustrations were dreamed up in 1494.

"In Mantegna's larger painting we have Parnassian dancing ladies, with beautiful limbs, and bodies, and indifferent faces."

"Perhaps the models were her ladies in waiting at the ducal court?" I asked Taylor.

"Perhaps. She also called to life a 'ladies' academy'—blue stockings like herself—perhaps they were 'the Parnassians' on the painting."

"Any more masters in her coterie?"

"Wrong expression," Taylor replied. "The artists of the Renaissance were free spirits. They accepted commissions, sponsorships or even gifts and grants. Think of Botticelli and the Medicis. But as far as we know, for the *Marchese*, the *objet d'art*, be it painting or sculpture, was more important than the artist. We have nearly two thousand letters from her in at least thirty public or private archives."

"And only one of them referring indirectly to Giorgione . . ."

"Only one of them extant," Taylor answered. "Yet, not everything has been totally explored. We know her contact with Leonardo, Raphael, Ariosto, Bocardo, Bembo, but what about the others? Take the Vatican archives with its 200,000 bound volumes. A given volume may have any number of items, a gathering of forty or fifty or even a hundred pieces. Only the top or cover names are systematically listed, in many cases the writers of the letters only, and not the recipients. As to the subjects of those letters? The list is a hit and miss."

"How could this be?" I wondered.

"Elementary, my dear Giorgio. The archives were *secret archives* until recently. Centuries of arcane deposits."

"Was there any sculpture of her visage, done while she was alive?"

"Yes, but I can't recall it, exactly. There was or there is a bust . . . I don't remember the sculptor, either."

Helena was spending hours and hours in her bedroom. In our Victorian terraced house, we have three bedrooms, a dining-living room and a breakfast room.

We had bought the house the year before, when Lucia Barbatella, Dad's maiden sister, died suddenly of a heart attack; her market gardening business was sold in Castelfranco, and the proceeds were shared out among the surviving siblings. Dad gave me the larger portion of his inheritance, which was more than enough for a house deposit.

Our double bed was in the master bedroom, a sofa and easel in the second bedroom, and the box-room was for guests. Truly, only one guest could fit in the little room. When entertaining a couple, we let them sleep on a pull-out bed in the living room.

Helena's room—the second bedroom—was the replica of her maiden room, the white "picture gallery". Since her operation she had not painted anything. For a while she did not eat, then ate only precooked food as she had no interest in the kitchen. We have a small back garden; she had planted flowers but entrusted the work of mowing to me. Birds from the sky came to her as they had come to St Francis of Assisi. Sparrows ate from her hand. Starlings bustled and jostled as she was spreading the seeds or the morsels on the feeding trays. Dinner remains were fed to the crows. She seemed the least unhappy when she was in the garden, but there are too many rainy days in London. One day I went to the garden centre and bought there two zebra finches—which she named Flutter and Fluttee.

Given my late June holiday and my parents' willingness to look after Flutter and Fluttee, I managed to persuade Helena to come with me to Ferrara. Dad had a childhood friend, one of the Baldi family, living in a comfortable cottage with his wife, just outside the ruins of the one-time city wall. We got a room there, the window looking out on to a vegetable garden. Baldi was a bony man with a rotund wife and two pet beagles around the house. In conversation I told him—which he must have known—that being a Barbatella I was a namesake of the painter.

"Not so," he said, raising his eyebrows. His name was *Barbarella*." I lost one of my illusions, or rather, my pretensions.

There was a direct flight to Bologna twice a week and a good railway link to Ferrara. As the coming and the going took one day, we had five more to discover the town, meet the Contessa and study her *Book of Hours*.

Of the many possibilities, Helena chose a guided tour from the Bay of Ferrara on the Adriatic to the estuary of the Po River. The ship chugged along the port, the beach, it went around the Isola dell' Amore and between Lo Scanno and the Sacca di Goro. Reaching il Taglio delle Falce and the canal which leads to Goro, we stopped to eat our packed lunch, observed the fishermen hauling in bream and eel, and—to Helena's delight—the birds that flew around and above us. She gave most of her lunch to the seagulls. I felt once more a desire to fish, as I had done as a boy, but which lack of time or opportunity had usually robbed me of since. Helena felt so attuned to nature that on each of the following Ferrara days she chose another ship-trip to other parts of the Ferrara land-sea-river and canalscape.

On the second day I met the Contessa. Before our Ferrara journey we had received her telephone number from Jirar, but when I called her she curtly said, "Ring me again, when you are in town—but never in the morning." I rang midday and arranged to meet her at the celebrated Piazza Ariostea, by the statue of the poet. She was ageless and very, very vivacious. She wore black lace gloves on her narrow, long-fingered hands and a two-tone silk dress down to her pinched ankles. She had a pearl necklace and an elongated diamond ring. She spoke Florentine—upper class Italian, slightly rolling her r's—and she was kind and smiling and open and most endearing.

She chattered about Biagio Rosetti, the Renaissance architect, his buildings, the Palazzo Diamonti and the Palazzo Massari—he was "*molto simpatico*" (very likeable), so were his *palazzi* and his sponsors, Ercole and his family. She never explained how she was related—directly or indirectly—to the Gonzaga, what was the source of her title, she being a Gonzaga and not an Este; why she lived in Ferrara, not in Mantua, and how she got hold of the wonderful "Gonzaga" *Book of Hours*. "I'll see you tomorrow," she said, in front of the nineteenth-century house of apartments where she rented an elegant flat on the second floor.

Next day I met her at a party organised in the Cafeteria del Castello Estense (a roomy hall recently transformed), which was regaled by the *literati*, and the other *cognoscenti*. Rather rudely, and transgressing the rules set down by Castiglione, I made a beeline to her. (She was in black evening dress, with a flowing black kerchief and a necklace, where encased small diamond globules were alternating with black pearls.)

"Caro Barba . . . hm . . . ella . . . nell . . . can I call you Giorgio?"

"By all means."

"Well, I tell you what: take me home; this little gathering will not last long."

"I'll accompany you, with pleasure, but then I cannot stay. I have another, a late appointment."

"Let that be. Come tomorrow after midday, around 1 P.M. Will you?"

"I will."

"I'll serve you brunch."

The brunch consisted of *vitello tonato*, egg mayonnaise, buns and sharon fruit.

We had to wash our hands before handling the little prayer book. It was bound in off-white vellum; the decorated leaves were of thick handmade paper, twelve leaves (or pages) to a gathering. *Duodecimo*. I held not a manuscript but a fabulously illuminated early printed book in my hand. According to its colophon, it was printed in Paris (printer unknown) on 17 February in 15?? The last two numbers of the date were heavily scored out. The sixty leaves (i.e. 120 illuminated pages) were 120 × 78mm in size, and the texture of the paintings on them was tempera. The binding had the Gonzaga crest. The Contessa poured out a cascade of information:

"Have you counted the lines?"

"Not yet."

"The text is presented in thirty-four lines per leaf. The contents are similar to other *Livre d'Heures,* insofar as it has a calendar, a passage of St John's Gospel, beginning *In principio erat Verbum,* followed by *Missus est angelus Gabriel,* St Luke I: 1–14; then *cum natus est Jesus in Bethlehem,* Matthew II: 1–12; then the sending out of the Apostles, Mark 16: 14–20; and a prayer to the Virgin Mary: *Observate . . .* which is followed by *Intemerata*—another prayer to Mary, and then the name giver: *Horae Beatae Mariae Virginis.* The last section contains seven penitential psalms, the Litany of All Saints, the *Officium de*

Cruce, and finally, the *Officium de Sancto Spirito.*"

All this was presented to me by her turning the pages. The condition of the book was excellent—apart from scored out lines.

I pondered and said, "I guess this book was commissioned by someone high and aristocratic, perhaps a ruler, whose portrait we might know from some picture gallery."

"You mean Isabella. I'd like to believe that, but I cannot yet prove it."

"May I ask its provenance?"

"Oh yes. I got it from my husband, Count Frederico Gonzaga, for our twentieth wedding anniversary."

"He has passed away, I presume."

"He has. He was the best man in the world, and ended up the poorest. In his younger days he inherited a palazzo in Mantua with all its furniture and chattels. This book was in the library room in a velvet covered case. I know nothing of its earlier history."

"Perhaps the representations of certain saints lead us nearer to a clue. We have St Bernard, St Benedict, St Francis of Assisi, St Claire and St Joseph, Mary's husband, appearing on certain leaves. On leaf 40, appearing with the three kings, he wears a red cloak, not dissimilar to the one he is wearing on Giorgione's *Holy Family* picture, to be found at the London National Gallery."

"Yes," she replied, "Jirar Azirjan has told me that already: he had examined both pictures and compared the two."

"So the Giorgione connection was his idea, was it?"

"Rather. I had told him I wanted to sell the book for a good price so that I could buy this flat for my old age."

"That is, surely, far away."

"Flattery will get you anywhere. What else can you discover when examining this book?"

I asked for time, and solitude, and sought her company again at 5 P.M. in the afternoon.

We had tea. The china set was Chinese, with a mandarin and his court on the cups and saucers. The *cuchiaini* (the little spoons) carried the Gonzaga crest. We had toast, rosehip jam, whipped cream and Lyons tea.

"Will you take cream or milk with it?"

"Neither, thank you. I prefer black tea."

After the tea and small talk—she had an excessive knowledge of opera and ballet—we washed our hands again (like Pilate), and picked up the book that glorifies Mary, the mother of Jesus Christ.

No doubt, and no matter who its miniaturist was, the illuminations of this early prayer book were exquisitely artistic—one might even say: top art. Textually and structurally, the *Book of Hours* was a late development of St Benedict's regulated prayers: the night's hour, the dawn's laudation, the morning prayer, the prayer at forenoon, the midday prayer, the afternoon prayer, the sunset prayer, the prayer before going to bed. Each of these is started with a florid initial complementing the margin, as it were, with acanthus leaves, green tendrils alternating with ochre and the red berries, where blue butterflies and skylarks dwelt. On leaf 38 there was a marginal bear and two goats; on 43 a stork; on 46 a small mammal riding on a snail; on 49 a dragon; on 58 a hybrid creature having a rabbit's body with a man's head. I didn't think that one could draw conclusions of specificity: most contemporary books of fables, dreams, and even representations of animals, contained creatures real or imaginary. There was also a veritable monster facing and gazing at the reader. (The treasure house of the imaginary beasts is the *Book of Kells*.)

Our *Libro d'Ore*, as the Contessa kept referring to her treasure, was prominent in one respect: the quality of its full-leaf paintings which showed the same hand and one unmistakable style. Apart from the visitation scene, already described, we had full-length miniatures of the *Ave Maria* (leaf 23), the Holy Family (leaf 41), St Joseph's dream (leaf 44) and the adoration of the Kings (leaf 48), the flight to Egypt (leaf 51), the Crucifixion (leaf 53) and the Whitsun gathering of the Apostles (leaf 59).

The other pictures, of saints, angels, shepherds, were marginals, or they were set inside the text as squares.

It is remarkable how often, and how relatively prominently, St Joseph occurred in the full-length pictures, and with what kind of representational unanimity. He was always an older man, with a baldish head and a long white beard. He always wore a red cloak and appears (presumably it was him—the features were telling) also in the Whitsun scene, with Mary and the Apostles.

The portrait of St Joseph in the *Adoration of the Shepherds* (Vienna, Kunsthistorisches Museum) shows a similar visage to that of our *libro*.

Mary, the mother of Jesus, has the same face throughout, the same gestures, and her clothing always contains an element of blue: blouse, cloak, headdress. One can have little doubt that the face of the Virgin was modelled on a real woman—perhaps living before the end or just after the turn of the fifteenth to sixteenth century; nor can we exclude the possibility that St Joseph and the Apostles were modelled on men living in the ambience of the painter.

"But who was he?" asked the Contessa.

"If we ever found a letter of commission we might then presume that it was Giorgione, or some other associate of his."

"And if not, or in the meanwhile?"

"There is a drawing attributed to the 'circle of Giorgione' showing the Holy Family where the kneeling Joseph is not dissimilar to the Joseph in your *libro*. A follower of Giorgione, Guilio Campagnola, drew a picture entitled *The Astrologer* where a curious monster also appears, not unlike the one to be found in your book. There may be other possibilities, but I can honestly say: no probabilities. Stylistic comparisons are not dominant, and without some documentary evidence we can say nothing concrete. Still, you have a marvellous *Libro d'Ore* illuminated by an unidentified artist, with great pictorial skill," I concluded.

(Before Giorgione, landscapes and figures had coexisted in the miniatures of the books of hours. Giorgione might have been encouraged by this idea when developing his own style.)

"One drinks for triumphs as well as for failures. I'll open a bottle of champagne."

"Only a glass for me . . ."

"I'll polish off the rest, don't worry."

5. Mantua

"If I could live again I would like to be the Duke of Mantua."
(The Duke of Wellington)

In the small back garden of 65, Gowan Avenue, Fulham, where we lived, Helena established a bird and hedgehog sanctuary. The birds now had three houses—they soon used one of them as a nest for brooding, breeding, teaching their fledglings to fly (we had some trouble with the neighbours' tabby cat)—and two elevated trays, on metal poles, which the cat could not climb. Meanwhile, the domesticated finches freely flew around the house, ate the morsels (they shouldn't have) from my saucer and kept on making love, now and again, and again and again. There were eggs galore—the size of a large bean—but none of them hatched. (One contained an underdeveloped dead chick.)

My dad continued to be as fit as a fiddle; my mum, on the other hand, had developed a slight weakness of the heart. We trusted Dr Watson no more, so I took her to the heart clinic in Charing Cross Hospital. She had to do exercises, ECG, sundry X-rays, and was diagnosed with a *slight* angina pectoris. Not enough to operate.

"What does *slight* mean?" I asked the consultant, a pretty young woman with thick black spectacles and loose black shoes.

"It means that she hasn't got a clear, even flow in one of her arteries. But the extent of her blockage cannot be diagnosed at once. She needs to take it easy and come back again in a month's time. Then we might do an arteriography."

"What might that be?"

"We pump a coloured liquid into her circulating blood which would help to show the narrowing of an artery or indeed might show a partial blockage."

This was done, as ordered. Then Mum had a blow-out of the tricky artery. She recovered well.

I was consulting with Peter Taylor regarding the *Book of Hours* and my progress in presenting and describing it.

He was satisfied, but put further probing questions to me, to himself, and indeed—by urging me to contact her again—to the Contessa.

"These *libri d'ore* were, on the whole, illuminated by unknown artists or, put it this way: artists whose identity could not be readily revealed. In the pre-Renaissance period, the habit of creating the books of hours, and reading them, was not unlike building cathedrals, whose architects are still, on the whole, unknown."

"Granted," I said. "But the Renaissance was to change all that, fundamentally. Alberti's influence radiated from building construction to such paintings, and sculptures, where we find signatures at the bottom of the canvas or initials such as A.D.— Albrecht Dürer, that is."

"Undoubtedly. But the custom of signing or initialling a miniature is, I think, unknown. What you have done in connection with the *libro* is enough for your MA, but it is not enough, I think, to satisfy your own curiosity."

"You are right about that, sir."

"Well then, pick up the pieces once again. That letter of the

Duchess of Ferrara to her agent Taddeo Albino, dated 20 October 1810 in Mantua, asks him about finding among the things of 'Zorzo', a picture of *'una nocte, molto bella et singulare'*. In other words, she was not asking Albino to commission Zorzo to paint such a picture for her—it must have already been painted, and she, at all accounts, must have already seen that, sometime, somewhere.

"In Albino's reply, on 8 November 1510, from Venice, he asserted that, among the pictorial remains of Giorgione, no such picture was found by the painter's associates since he had died of the plague.

"No one said, or claimed, that *'una nocte'* had not existed. But if it had existed, and because Zorzo was highly esteemed in his lifetime, and even more appreciated since, the picture must still exist, somewhere."

"Must is a strong word," I said. "There were wars, lootings, conflagrations on Italian soil, between the 1500s and the 1980s. It could have been sold surreptitiously to an English lord or acquired by force by a German officer during World War II. Nonetheless, the matter deserves further investigation, particularly since art galleries, their custodians or other art historians, starting with Vasari, cannot give us any further lead."

"Contessa Gonzaga . . . or any other private person among her relatives or friends or acquaintances . . . Wouldn't she, wouldn't they have a lead?"

"I don't even know her Christian name."

"Ask your friend, the Milan antiquarian."

I wrote to Jirar Azirjan soon after my consultation with Taylor and by return of post received his reply: the Contessa was called Fatima.

I wrote to her about *"una nocte"*, sending, at the same time, a Christmas card of the silent night outside the stable, the adoration of the kings, shepherds and all inside the stable. In other words—a postcard reproduction of Titian's painting.

No reciprocation.

Months later I sent her an Easter Card, with the painting of *Parnassus* by Mantegna, reproduced not bigger than palmsized. And I had the temerity to mention my Christmas card, not reciprocated.

Meanwhile, I was pondering: how was it that Vasari, the source of the lion's share of knowledge about Giorgione, put his hero's death at 1511? And why do respectable art historians—some 10 per cent of all—claim that the painter was born in 1478?

The Contessa phoned me after Easter. "I have not received your Christmas card," she said in her strong voice on the telephone. She was charming and helpful once again. Yes, she knew a picture, which was being deliberately hidden from the world and could easily be christened *"una nocte"*.

"Where? Who owns it? May I humbly ask?"

"My late husband's brother-in-law: Annibale Ammanati has it."

"One of the Florentine Ammanatis?" (The rhyme ran through my mind: *Ammanati, Ammanati, che bel marmo rovinati*—you've ruined a lovely piece of marble.)

"Yes, but he lives in Mantua. To be precise, in a little village outside Mantua, called Caviana."

"Forgive me, I've never heard of it. Where is that?"

"Well, it is some ten kilometres north of Mantua. A typical Lombardian village."

"Has he a telephone number?"

"He has, but does not like to let strangers have it. They have to phone his sons, the conveyers of management. Or you have to write him a polite letter, and send a stamped addressed envelope."

I had some Italian stamps, so was able to begin the opening round of correspondence. The address: *Annibale Ammanati, Caviana, near Mantua, Lombardy, Italy,* proved sufficient.

In his answer Signor Ammanati offered hospitality in early July, for the two of us, in his sizeable guest house, situated at the edge of his stud farm. It wasn't free or cheap, but I booked it for a week. In his concluding letter, he pointed out the existence of the daily ride, hoping that both of us would take part in it.

Jirar had promised to pick us up by car in the Aeroporto Leonardo da Vinci in Milan, and then take us to Caviana, but only Jana waited for us at the airport. Jirar had a heavy cold, so she took us to the railway station, then returned to the city of Milan to nurse her friend. We took the train to Mantua, reaching it in the afternoon, and overnighted at the Albergho Gonzaga. We took an extended walking tour to the Palazzo Ducale, the Castello di San Giorgio, the Duomo (which was closed) and had a meal in the bar Charles Baudelaire, where we ate *frutta di mare*.

Helena discovered that apart from the double opening to Lake Garda, seven rivers, large, small and smaller, cut through the Mantuan territory. "May I come back, one day, while you are doing your research in Caviana?"

Next morning we took a bus which dropped us at the main square of the village at 11 A.M., and then walked a kilometre or so to the Ammanati stud farm.

Annibali Ammanati was in a paddock, whip in hand, engaged in breaking in a black horse. With his whip he signalled us to wait. The horse was a mare, bucking and rearing; Alfredo, the younger of the two Ammanati boys, sat firmly on her back and balanced his body expertly. The horse's mouth was foaming, her back wet, but the whip in Annibale's hand only cracked and danced in front of the mare's eyes; it did not touch her.

"We need three, sometimes four sessions," said Ammanati senior. "I'll lead you up to your room." I saw the horse consuming sugar cubes taken from Alfredo's hand.

In England I'd call this set-up a B & B, or a guest house; they called it *casa dei forestieri*. It was a two-level, square, nineteenth-century building, with five sizeable bedrooms, bathrooms, one large kitchen, salon and dining room downstairs. There were no TV sets in the bedrooms, but a very large one stood downstairs in the living room. Every evening the room filled with the noise of broadcasts. Communal enjoyment, for the merry and the bored.

This guest house was a replica of another building, the Casa Ammanati, which must have been at least 150 years older. In between the two there was a rose garden, well tended, with a fountain with a fawn in the middle, surrounded by a little pool with goldfish frolicking in it.

"Not one bird around," said Helena sadly.

Later we learned that Ammanati and his sons, Alfredo and Amedeo, were keen shots, and they never missed the *Festa degli uccelli*, the day when even songbirds could be hunted down and roasted on spits, legally.

Helena composed a poem in two stanzas, entitled: *Recipes.*

1. *Per la festa degli uccelli*
Take ten birds: a turkey, a goose, a duck,
a hen, a pheasant, a ptarmigan,
a woodpigeon, a nightingale, a blackbird
and a canary. Put all of them in a

cauldron with hot water then
spike their bodies with bacon, putting
their heart and giblets aside. Toss
the entrails to pigs. Roast the birds
on spits, and thus obtain skin
fast browning, soft meat, good
taste at the feast of the birds.

2. *Per la festa degli umani*

Take ten specimens: one from USSR, USA,
China, Hinduland, Arabia, Africa, Japan,
Israel, Albania and Czechoslovakia.
Don't put them in a cauldron, they have little hair.
Feed their entrails to the pigs. Sell
their heart, liver and lungs to hospitals
as transplantable bio-organs.
Tie them up, head and foot
like rams or young calves. Place
on this side of the spit the Arab and African,
they need less roasting, they are black already.
On the far side the small ones could hang,
less roasting is needed for the Israeli,
and the Czechoslovak. Human flesh is sweet.
The vultures will peck at it at the feast of the humans.

Next day, straight after breakfast—which was good, healthy,
and included an optional cup of *kumis*—we were invited to join
the daily ride. Apart from us there were two more couples staying in the guest house, and a young man of about thirty. He was
a friend of the Ammanati boys.

After breakfast Helena disappeared like camphor. Before
taking French leave, she whispered to me: "I'll discover those

rivers and some of the towns. I will be back tonight, before dark." It was an agreement between us that she would always return to base—wherever she goes—before dark.

Ammanati was a tall, lean man, dressed always in black, and touching a bushy black moustache. His speech was sputtering like a candle and crackling like dry wood in fire. I told him that I had never sat on a horse before, except once in a circus where my mount, a grey pony, was led around the ring.

"No matter, my friend. It is free and very healthy. On horseback you are a different man. And all we do, anyway, is go around, like a convoy, this small estate of 110 acres. Amedeo will look after you."

Around we went. At one side the riding route bordered a small forest, at the end of which I spotted a badger hole. We also circled the paddock, the two stables and yards, a clump of rhododendron bushes and a small stream. Amedeo warned us: "My horse will jump across, but you need not imitate me." We didn't. We waded in and walked through.

The group stopped at the fountain, where Annibale commented: "The ride was free, but as you dismount you may contribute to the upkeep of the cloister near by and drop your coins in the pool." We did. At sunset an elderly nun appeared and fished out the money, leaving the goldfish undisturbed.

"You need a couple of lessons," Annibale told me, "then you can go on the advanced ride."

"I am not sure I want the advanced ride . . ."

"But you want to look at my treasure, the picture, don't you? I won't show it to a greenhorn."

I had a lesson in the afternoon, after having lunch at the village pub. Alfredo sat on his own horse, I sat on mine, he called out command words and performed the prescribed tasks, which included prodding the horse to canter, sudden stops, trotting—which I found pretty uncomfortable. I was glad when the lesson was over.

"It will be ten thousand liras," said the father, who had been keeping an eye on us. I paid. (I am writing these lines in 2006 as a recollection. My riding lesson took place in the summer of 1988 when 10,000 lira was about £5, the cost of a superb dinner at the time.)

After I washed and changed, the sun was setting, and Helena had not returned. The minutes passed as greyness set in and my concern increased, and by 9 P.M. it turned into vexatious anxiety. *Atra cura,* says Horace. Should I ask my hosts to give me a lift to town, and if so where would I look for her in Mantua? I was composing a line in my mind to ask the people on the street, the tourist guides (should I come across one) or the policemen: *Have you seen a tallish, fair woman with a Madonna face? She has long hair tied up on a crown on the top of her head. She is wearing white sandals and a white cotton dress just about covering her knees. She is Czech but speaks perfect Italian . . ."*

By the time I put all this together, a taxi stopped in front of the paddock, and Helena rushed out to embrace me.

I paid the driver.

She explained: "I went on the seven rivers tour; we crossed the Tartaro, the Tiene, the Secchia, the Oglio, the Chiese, the Mincio and ended up on the mighty Po. When we got back to Mantua, the last bus had already left for Caviana. There was no taxi in sight, just a telephone box. I did not know the phone number of this farm, yet I wanted to warn you. The only number I knew by heart was my mum's. I rang her. She rang Jana. Jana rang Jirar. Jirar rang the Contessa. The Contessa knew the

Ammanati number, and told my mother. But when she rang back, an empty taxi appeared in front of the Palazzo Ducale, so I hopped in, and here I am."

"How about coming with me to the neighbouring forest tomorrow?"

"Will you not go with the daily ride?"

"I'll skip that. And anyway, I'll be taking an advanced riding class in the afternoon. I would do best if you watched me."

Ammanati was quite satisfied with me and invited us for supper.

"How much would that cost?" I asked suspiciously.

"*Amicizia!* Aren't you Italians? A minor nobleman invites his compatriot for a family meal, cooked by his daughter-in-law."

The day went by agreeably. I showed the badger hole to Helena (there were two cavities with scratchings and with traces of paws). We found two squirrels climbing up a fir tree, a very hard and enormous petrified mushroom, and a fox, transfixed for a minute by the light of the lamp we carried, on a pathway, then slinking away rapidly, drawing his red tail behind him as if it were a burning torch.

Her favourites the birds weren't there. We were approaching an ageing oak tree with a carving on its trunk. And then, suddenly: hush! A snow owl broke out from its lair flailing his huge snow-white wings. Helena was mesmerised and fascinated.

"Oh," she said. "Oh, Oh."

The supper was simple and the company thawed out from its daytime stiffness. The polenta was tasty, the meatballs were well seasoned, the grapes were sweet.

Annibale spoke: "I believe our ancestors, I mean the Romans, kept horses here, two thousand years ago. Those horses were already domesticated. Their forebears were the tarpan, the real wild horses. The strongest horses came from Mongolia: I have a couple of the Przewalski horses whose ancestry could be traced back to Mongolia."

The lady of the house, Alfredo's wife Pia, a slight, silent, house-proud lady and an excellent cook, quietly spoke up: "Whose turn is it?"

The tall, proud, stiff-necked master of the house stood up, went to the kitchen and dealt with the dirty dishes.

"We have a rota system," said Alfredo.

I turned to Amedeo: "Your father is keen on the ancestry of his horses but has not yet informed me of his, of your family connection with the Gonzaga."

"Simple," said Amedeo. "The Ammanati can trace their ancestry back to the sixteenth-century sculptor. They were artisans and small landowners then. My dad married my late mother, herself Contessa Lucrezia Gonzaga, the younger sister of Frederico III, Fatima's husband. While Frederico wasted almost all his inheritance, my mother's tiny estate, our 110 acres, was maintained by Dad, who established a stud farm here, now as old as I am."

I guessed that the Ammanati brothers were around the same age as me but a little older than Helena.

When Annibale has finished the washing up he joined us, offering Strega to everyone. My inquisitiveness continued, and he became a little more talkative.

"Tell me about the Contessa in Ferrara. How does she fill up her time? I was her guest not so very long ago, but she gave nothing away at that time."

"She is writing her memoirs. She was a fairly well-known ballerina in Milan—part of the La Scala set-up—but she performed far and wide in Italy and danced in France, Germany and Holland."

"When?"

"If I told you that you could guess her age, and that is a state secret. Anyway, to cut it short, one day Frederico saw her in *Swan Lake*. After the performance, he surprised her with an avalanche of lilies, and after six months courtship, married her. Then they lived like a pair of gloves for many years until cancer of the liver robbed her of him."

"May I know a bit about the *Nocte?*"

"How many riding lessons have you had? I believe only two. You are still a novice horseman. I have to see you taking Pegasus at full flight in the straights and jump across the stream, landing faultlessly; then we can talk about the picture."

Next day I rode again. Helena explored the Palazzo Ducale and the Casa del Mantegna. She called my attention to the splendidly regaled Pegasus of Mantegna's *Parnassus*, a copy of which hung there since the original was in the Louvre. The horse seemed to be kissing his carer. Annibale transported his horse, Bucefalo, to a flat race in Milan that day; it was the Prix Ambrosiana; he won. So Annibale was in an excellent mood that evening.

"Tomorrow, after your last lesson, we can look at my *Nocte*."

I remembered the difficulties in viewing Cavallini's *Cena* in a convent of Santa Cecilia in Rome. I had to get up at 5 A.M., knock on the door at 5.30 A.M., be admitted by the verger on tiptoes, and see the mural while the nuns—under strict *clausara*—were having their breakfast at a distance from the painting, which showed Christ having His supper with the apostles.

Late that afternoon Annibale called on me. From the large

living room we—opening a padlock—entered a small chamber, without a window or any visible lighting. Then on the wall opposite he switched on a picture light under which, beveiled, lived the picture. When he drew the curtain and my eyes got accustomed to the picture light, I spotted the *Nocte* with its internal illumination, by its own moonlight and a small bundle-wood fire. I could begin to discover and discern what the painting represented. The picture, with frame and all, was not *on* the wall; it was embedded, *built in* the wall, and was protected by unbreakable glass.

"I can't even see the picture properly."

"You see that shelf with my magnifier on it? A small periscope, if you please. Use it."

I did. It was so strong that I could even discern the granules of oil paint. It was thickly laid in both front corners: the crown of a huge oak tree, on the right, was enveloped into thickening darkness, the dark green transcribed into blackish blue. The foliage of the visible corner of the copse on the other side was already blackish blue, and it merged into light blackness. A young lutist supported his red-coated back against the bulk of the oak tree; the beam of the half-moon visible between two dark-grey clouds in the sky darted right on to the scene. The lute, although tiny, was well discernable, the wench listening to it likewise. She was propped up on her right elbow, her face turned towards the lutist (her lover? her friend? her musician?), her naked feet just about visible from under the folds of her long red skirt. She wore a white blouse, and her brown hair fell forward on her right shoulder, complementing her face of a lighter hue.

On the opposite side, in front of the corner of the copse, a man was attending a small bundle-wood fire. He was crouching and, with a piece of brushwood in hand, was stoking the fire.

The flames painted his face red and made his skin—for he was naked to the waist—almost equally red. Helena asked, then was granted permission, to come to see the picture.

"Pure poetry," she said, barely audibly, as if under a spell.

"You want to know how I got hold of it, don't you?" said Annibale, twisting his moustache. "It was Frederico's. You know that Isabella the Great had over 1,500 *objets d'art*—some inherited, left and right, most disappeared (even stolen) without a trace. Now only this picture, the *Book of Hours* and a third, a female nude, remained with a branch of the family.

"In order to settle a huge gambling debt, Frederico sold the nude to me. It was a signed picture by Dosso Dossi. He showed a well-proportioned lady with golden contours. One day a guest cunningly spirited it away. The picture hung in the parlour just above the disused fireplace. He had arranged a small conflagration in the smaller of the two stables. Arson. We all ran out to quench the fire, and he ran away with the picture, not to be seen ever again."

"Was it a listed painting, known to the International Commission?"

"Indeed. Perhaps it is now decorating the vaults of some American millionaire."

"And the *Nocte*?"

"It is not a listed painting. In his dotage, and winning on the horses, Frederico threw an open air party on a fleet of ships in Mantua. *Navigazione fluviale*. To square the prodigal party of enormous costs—it was also his seventieth birthday—he gave me this picture, and I paid his party bill. Learning from my misfortune with the Dossi nude, I built a practically unbreakable nest around the *Nocte*."

"*Nocte*, night scene," I was thinking aloud. "Giorgione has a more-or-less authenticated painting, *The Three Philosophers*, which—perhaps because the air suggests sunset—some critics call nocturnal. But if so, then *The Astrologer* exudes the same vision of the rays of the departing sun in the background accentuated by the mother in white and her naked child, skin-colour white in the forefront. But this *Nocte* of Ammanati has a truly analogous landscape all around."

"It has. And although I cannot show it to you, the verso of the panel on which it was painted has an inscription: 'ILL.MA et EXC.MA ISABELLA DUCHESSA D'ESTE'."

"An ownership mark, I presume. But apart from that, and Isabella's desire to own '*una nocte*' by Giorgione—which Albino could not find at the time—there is no indication that Isabella had wished to acquire this particular picture, as this is not signed, nor seen, nor authenticated by experts."

"We are amateurs, my sons, my daughter-in-law and I. The nearest half-expert I know, but not well enough, is your friend, the antique shark, Jirar Azirjan. I know he and Fatima want to market her last treasure: the *Libro d'Ore*."

"Which is also an unauthenticated work of an early sixteenth-century artist. When I saw it, last year, I thought that its miniaturist had deliberately hidden his identity. Since then I saw a book of hours which belonged to the Duc du Berry, and it was definitely executed by the Limburg brothers."

Helena had suddenly piped up: "This is what I think: once in the past Isabella had seen and loved a painting, called *Una Nocte* by Zorzo. He died, and the painting could not be located. Then she asked another, perhaps Antonio Allegri da Correggio, to paint the night scene. Isabella had a sharp eye and would have remembered the details of the lost *Nocte*. Correggio could have obliged to paint a likeness."

It is a beautiful idea, I thought, and raised no audible objections. Correggio's treatment of light and darkness is exemplary in his *Holy Night*. He was the rage of connoisseurs at the beginning of the nineteenth century, then his fame somewhat faded. (Helena was still a Correggio Madonna, and she knew it.)

"Signor Ammanati," I said, "there is a technique for investigation which requires no physical contact with the painting. Fluorescent spectroscopy. It identifies chemical elements present at the surface of the painting."

"It might do, but it cannot distinguish, I believe, between the delicate brushstrokes of Correggio, Giorgione or—for that matter—Leonardo. Moreover, it would open my secret to the gaping art historians, the gazing public. No, I don't want that," he replied.

"Well, then, what I am going to say will only be of academic interest. There is a technique of chemical examination of paint and organic binding agents. Using gas chromatography coupled with mass spectrometry, the investigators, using a small globule of *La Vecchia*'s veil, concluded that Giorgione had mixed dull ochre and more opaque red ochre with lead white."

"Stop it, signor. No one will touch my painting."

Of course, I stopped, and only in thought referred to the fact that *Nocte* is not just an ordinary night scene, it is a *Nativity*. A picture of the birth of Jesus.

6. Prague

"Truth will triumph."
(Jan Hus)

"The Aztecs believed in the supernatural nature of the horse."
(Per Olafson)

I got my MA and soon an advancement: I was appointed assistant lecturer in the History of Art department at University College. The small extra salary had eased our financial situation. I translated a number of Italian articles into English, to make ends meet—the mortgage was crippling. We not infrequently ate at La Bocca, free of charge (Mamma's arrangement), and at her place, likewise.

I begged her to take it easy, even though she had no new symptoms and her heart was working regularly. Dad had received a lump sum in early retirement money, and he put down £3,000 towards our mortgage payments.

Helena lived in a dream world. One day she picked a multitude of wild flowers in Bishop's Park and decorated every room of our house with them.

"It is lovely," I said. "But what's the occasion?"

"The Prince of Wales is coming for tea with his *new* bride," she answered. I did not know he had one.

"And what will you serve them?"

"I believe she favours Twinings tea and simple honey cakes."

She baked about a hundred Czech honey cakes, all heart shaped. The royals had other arrangements. We kept on munching the honey cakes for two weeks.

Another time she put on her best evening dress, in the afternoon, just as I was coming home from work. A velvet poem of a black frock with a white Brussels lace collar, and similar turn-back cuffs. She did look like a born princess, but we did not have a princely invitation, or a visit.

Was it fantasy or was it play? I entered into the play, as Prince Giorgio Niccolò Barbatella, ruler of Castelfranco, temporarily exiled to Fulham, London, England.

"But *I am* an exiled princess, from Prague!" Helena said. "My uncle Prince Jaroslav usurped the throne of my father, King Pavel, and I and my mother were chased away to an enchanted island. Here the beer is warm, like slosh, the butter is salty, the fork is held inside out at meals, and people are not expected to greet their elders but must wait until they are greeted first."

I replied: "I am also an exiled marquis, whose rightful inheritance of three Giorgione pictures: *The Portrait of Caterina Carnaro*; *The Portrait of Laura,* and the *Madonna with the Infant Jesus and Saint John* was robbed of him and hidden in unknown places. The fourth was a man in the nude, with his back turned and his feet plunged into a limpid stream of water bearing his reflection. To one side was a burnished cuirass that the man had taken off, and this reflected his left profile (since the polished surface of the armour revealed everything clearly); on the other side was a mirror reflecting the other profile of the nude figure."

In the late autumn of 1989 I was working on a project, for the students, which I was to put into practice next autumn: The

Ten Artists. (I'll give an account of it later because momentous events interrupted the slow-paced trundle of our lives' movements.)

"Freedom, Giorgio, freedom!" shouted Helena as soon as I entered the front door of our house. She jumped on me, hugged me, hung on my breast for minutes.

Somehow, my mind being engaged with other things, I hadn't noticed that the fearful giant, the Soviet Union, had buckled and was on its knees. All of a sudden, in a matter of days, weeks—and regarding Romania, in months—the east European satellite countries broke free.

"Czechoslovakia is no more a people's democracy, it is a democracy!" said she, still animated and running for her drawing pad. On it—we went into the bedroom—was the pencil drawing of a castle, which I could not recognise, which she had done from memory. "The royal castle in Prague," she said, her lithe body still glued to me.

"But you have not seen it, have you? You were only two years old when you left Prague."

"Mama has seen it, Jana has seen it, I have seen photos and paintings of it, and from time to time I see it in my dreams."

"So you want to go back, and see it with me in reality?" I knew that an experience is sealed for posterity if shared between two people who love each other deeply.

"Can we? Can we scrape up enough money?"

I thought of Maria, Jana, Jirar and a car trip. "I think we can."

And it happened; what all so rarely happens happened again, at her initiative. She provoked intimacy, which turned out to be as stormy as our encounter in the gondola in Venice was.

Telephone calls to Wimbledon (Maria), to Genoa (Jana), to Milan (Jirar) concluded in agreement. Helena and I were to fly from Heathrow to Milan, Leonardo da Vinci Airport, accompanied by, and paid for by Maria. The three of us were to be picked up in Milan by Jirar and Jana, and crossing middle Europe with Jirar's five-seater Mercedes, we would overnight in Salzburg. All went fine. Sitting in the front seat, I was still able to absorb a lesson in modern Czech history delivered from the back seat by the two sisters, both animated. Helena, sitting in between her mother and aunt, kept on interrupting them with excited questions.

"Were Benes and Masaryk two such brainboxes?"

The answer was a laudation of these two Czechoslovak lodestars. I kept quiet, but thought that these two theoreticians must have been the Peter and Paul of Czechoslovak unity. Then came schisms: one enforced by the Germans, the other coming much later in 1993. If you had a small country, why not make it miniscule? There are some fools in northern Italy who would cut the heritage of Caesar and of Garibaldi into two lame units.

Well, at the time of our journey the rise of Václav Havel was on the cards. Jana knew him personally. Maria had read some of his plays. Helena had heard of his fortitude, and of Charta 77, an initiative that presaged the Velvet Revolution of 1989.

After Salzburg—and a whiff of the Alps—we drove straight to Prague and there encamped in Hotel Amadeus. It was a modest place, halfway between the Ritz and a scout tent. Jirar excused himself that in the rush to book a hotel for Christmas he could not find a really decent one. Normally quite talkative, he was very quiet in Prague, and leaving the Merc with Jana, he disappeared for four days.

With Maria's guidance, we went to the White Unicorn café

where Kafka used to hang out and, while at the German university, Einstein too.

"Wasn't there a famous painter who also frequented the place?" I asked the woman.

"There was, Oskar Kokoschka," said Jana. "And I met his lover too, the famous Alma Mahler."

The women, in their delight of freedom, and homecoming, weren't really missing Jirar. Helena, whose Czech was minimal, had bought herself a grammar, a dictionary and a guidebook. Since the guidebook was in Czech and most of the inscriptions, descriptions, labels and signs in the streets were too, I relied on her guidance.

We went everywhere by car—parking was not yet a problem—starting with Hradcany, the largest royal castle (so they claim) in Europe. Something like 500 something, something metres long. In it are chapels, galleries, rooms (fitted for no longer existing kings), courtyards, museums, but not enough toilets. A town in itself, perhaps comparable to the Vatican in size. But the hero of the Czechs—we admired his statue—is someone who once wanted to break away from the Catholic Church, Jan Hus.

"That faithless bastard"—Helena rarely used swear words—"Emperor Sigismund burnt him at the stake." It was a strange ejaculation from a Catholic girl. We visited Karolineum and saw the statue of Hus in front it, proud, defiant. Helena asked if I could understand the inscriptions encapsulating the motto of Jan Hus. I couldn't. Then she spelt it out in English: *Truth will triumph!*

Another day we went to the National Museum, and while looking down at Wenceslas Square from the vast collections of minerals held in parallel rooms, we lost sight of Maria and Jana. Down in the square festivities loomed large. As the snow began to fall in thin flakes, some people opened their mouths to welcome the cold refresher; others, wearing fur hats and gloves, thronged around chestnut-roasting fires and watched small rockets spluttering firework stars. Some climbed up towards the gathering snow clouds, while a clump of kids sang "Good King Wenceslas". Helena, as if in a trance, let my hand go and ran down to the square.

I followed but lost her, so I sat down on the steps outside the main door of the museum. *Che sarà sarà.* First her aunt, then her mother appeared, with a well-dressed gentleman wearing a Burberry coat. He was introduced to me as Dr Emil Hacha jr, an old friend of, indeed a school friend of, Maria's. Now we were four, and at my suggestion we split the distance equally and thus combed St Wenceslas Square. We found Helena in a corner, sitting on a pallet, drawing (absolutely absorbed) on the end papers of her books. There was the tower clock drawn neatly, with a tiny dancing girl at its minute hand, the newspaper kiosk, with a wreath of people linked up arm in arm with one another, and a large bunch of Michaelmas daisies. Despite their sympathies for the "heretic" Hus, my three ladies were Catholics, and so was Emil Hacha, who accompanied us to St Ursula's church for midnight mass. I enjoyed the carols.

Next day, early in the morning, Helena and I walked out to the river at Karl Bridge. As the mist lifted so did the wings of a flock of swans, the swish filling the air for a second. We went to the cathedral to an evening concert; the proverbially reserved Czechs were talkative, bubbly, and we knew that we were part of making history but did not know that it was to be called the Velvet Revolution.

On 28 December, Jirar Azirjan returned—from where? Was it a secret?

"No secret," said Jana at the airport. "He is coming back from Famagusta."

"From the Turks or from the Greeks?" asked I again in an asinine manner. Because everyone knows that although Greeks as well as Turks live in Cyprus, they live more or less in separate enclaves, and an Armenian gentleman like Azirjan could not have frequented the company of Turks, whom his ancestors had escaped from.

And then, there he was, carrying three bouquets of flowers, while a luggage porter carried his trunk and placed it in the back of the white Merc. We were to drive back to the hotel, then next day, back to Milan, the same way we had come.

Yet another surprise: Maria stayed on in Prague. "Just for another week," she said to Helena. With the vibes of a daughter and the instinct of a woman, Helena knew that her mother had met someone—or met someone again—who was responsible for her change of heart, her change of direction. It was Emil Hacha, the middle-aged son of a one-time diplomat, someone she knew as a schoolgirl knows a schoolboy, and then knew him as her late husband's colleague. Far from being taken aback, Helena readily excused her mother; and later when Maria had just announced her intention to remarry, she gave her her blessing.

"Mama had a blissful marriage to my father when she was young. Later she had a marriage of convenience, with no emotions involved. Now, at the age of fifty, she fell in love—not only with a man from Prague but with beautiful Prague again. I wished her well."

We did not attend the wedding that summer in Prague. Helena was pregnant again, in her eighth month in June. The baby was due at the beginning of July.

When I took Helena's three drawings, later enlarged and coloured, to Mr Corwen in Harrods, he recounted his recent experiences in eastern Europe. He spent a few days in the autumn by Lake Balaton in Hungary, more or less surrounded by East German tourists. One day, instead of going home to East Germany, they noisily forged their way to the West, via Austria. The Hungarians had opened the floodgates. Later, Mr Corwen was present at the demolition of the Berlin Wall, and brought home several small pieces, one of which he sent to Helena through the good offices of his daughter, Tatyana.

"We might have an independent Ukraine too," he said with more resignation than joy.

At the beginning of the last term of the 1989/1990 university year, I set an ambitious task to my ten students doing History of Art. "Each of you should select an Italian Renaissance painter working in the calendar year 1510." I recommended that each one of them would choose one painter from the following ten: Leonardo da Vinci, Giovanni Bellini, Giorgione da Castelfranco, Sandro Botticelli, Michelangelo Buonarroti, Titian, Antonio Correggio, Raphael, Sebastiano del Piombo and Lorenzo Lotto.

"Sir," piped up the talented but impertinent Mike Blood. He had flaming red hair, like one in ten of the Irish, betraying Viking origins. "There'll be a tumult for the grand masters; Leonardo, Michelangelo, Raphael are everyone's favourites. But who wants a second rate mannerist like Lotto?"

"All right, Mike. We will do it this way: the names of the painters will be placed in Imogen's red cap. Then the ten of you will pick a name one by one."

"Only nine," said Mike.

Imogen, a spectacularly tall and lean girl who was usually

wearing a dirndl and an apron, made a bid: "The owner of the red cap can start the round." She did, and got Botticelli.

"Now, your task is twofold. Everyone must do research to discover her or his painter's activity/or activities—or, for that matter, passivity—during the year 1510. When ready, or if you encounter insurmountable difficulties, you consult me. This is phase one, for which you will have four weeks. Then, in the second phase, you link up with that master—his researcher or researchers among you ten—who had associated with your charge in 1510 or could have done so, because master and master, or master and pupil knew one another. Having got that far, you then ought to look at as many paintings (or reproductions) of the linked-up artists, and determine (or just propose) to name the characteristic signs showing influence or interaction, or stylistic or semantic references of the age, of the trend of the region they prefer."

Tatyana, Helena's friend and Corwen's daughter, was one of the ten. She was a petite girl with jet black hair and well-carved bony hands and toes. Tatyana wore sandals, and I could not help noticing that all her toes moved, indeed pranced independently in her sandals. As luck would have it, her charge was Giorgione. She made interesting observations: "Big or small, all of Zorzo's figures were well or relatively well built. Even *La Vecchia* possessed a round body under a furrowed face."

Tatyana pointed out—although this was outside her remit—that Dürer painted an old woman looking not unlike *La Vecchia* in 1508 in Venice.

"Was this, or were the two, an allegory of avarice?"

"In frontal representations of nude women Giorgione," said Tatyana, "either covered up the most private part (as on *Venus*) or he painted the pubic hair. This custom was either unknown at his time or very rare (*La Tempesta*).

"Indeed, Michelangelo, Bellini and Botticelli always painted hairless pudenda. Tatyana also observed that on all the known paintings or prints based on paintings of Giorgione, only one horse ever featured. Yet the horse was the most frequent animal appearing on Renaissance paintings, before birds and dogs.

I told her, in private as it were, that I saw a small white horse on a painting—that might possibly be attributed to Giorgione, or a follower—in private possession. I was referring to Annibale Ammanati's *Nocte*. Furthermore, I called her attention—in the course of a seminar, with the other nine students present—to a section of Vasari's description of Giorgione's life and works, where he assuredly mentions a representation, perhaps a portrait of Caterina Cornaro, the Queen of Cyprus, on horseback.

Cyprus brought Jirar Azirjan to mind, and one evening I wrote him a letter:

31 May 1990

"Dear Jirar,

I know so very little about yourself apart from the antiques and antiquarian connection, and your friendship with Jana. With this letter I am aiming to extend my little knowledge of you. Excuse my curiosity.

Let me start by thanking you, once again, for your repeated hospitality to us, to my wife and me, without which we could have accomplished definitely less than we did.

Recalling the time in Prague, last Christmas, I was surprised by your sudden departure just before

Christmas Eve, and gratified by your return after the feast days of Christmas. Yet you were non-communicative on the way back, and markedly sadder than at the time of our departure for eastern Europe. You may think me too inquisitive—I don't deny the trait—and of course you might not wish to answer such personal questions.

Let me, therefore, move on to the professional field. You must know about Caterina Cornaro. Is she remembered or celebrated in Cyprus? Is there a visage of her still extant in the island? She was queen there in the fifteenth century and—according to Vasari—her portrait was painted by Giorgione on her return to Venice.

Finally, an offer. A friend of mine recently visiting Hungary picked up a map, 60 × 50cm, in Paris. The left top corner has the following information: ROYAUME DE HONGARIE, PRINCIPAVTE TRANSILVANIAE, SCLAVONIE, VALAQUIE . . . par le Sr. Robert, geographe ordinaire du Roi.

Avec Privilège, 1752.

Would this interest you, professionally? (GB)"

A fortnight later I had my reply from Jirar Azirjan:

14 June 1990

"My dear Giorgio,

Thank you for your kind letter. I am not put out by your inquisitiveness, and in answering you, I shall be as open and informative as I can be.

Between my departure from and return to Prague, I spent a few days in Famagusta, the place of my birth. My mother and father were refugees from Turkey where, in 1915–1916, on the pretext of World War I, the Turks killed about a million and a half Armenians. All out of spite and envy. I recommend that you read *The 40 days of Musa Dagh*—which—although a novel, conveys the atmosphere of those horrors, those terrible days. My dad and mam were a young engaged couple and lucky enough to escape to a peaceful island. There they married, and I was born, in 1920. A year later my younger brother, Tigran, was born. We grew up separately; I ended up in Milan, Tigran stayed in Cyprus, married there, had two children, and now has two grandchildren as well. He has a furniture shop and a comfortable house in Famagusta.

Yes, there in the museum at my birthplace we can find a statue of Queen Caterina; she stands on a pedestal, looking down. I guess it was sculpted in the nineteenth century. I don't know its sculptor.

In the 1920s and 1930s there were many, many Armenians in Cyprus, and even today there is a community numbering several thousand. When, after the Second World War, I managed to locate an undamaged Hellenistic statue of Venus (or Aphrodite) and—somewhat circuitously—sold it to the Metropolitan Museum in New York, I halved my profit, and together with some Cypriot Armenian merchants, established the Famagusta children's hospital. My brother at that time—a grown-up young man—developed duodenal cancer. I made a vow at the St Joseph altar of the Famagusta

Armenian Church that I would give, every year, half of the profit of my takings to the hospital. I did not say in my prayers that "if my brother recovers", God should not be held to ransom. But he did recover, and has been welcoming me every Christmas.

Among my doctor friends in Famagusta, there is a famous cancer specialist. You might have noticed that I walk with a slight limp—although I've been trying to hide it. My doctor friend, Eseian, diagnosed bone cancer in my right leg. I will, indeed, have radiation, and chemotherapy—and will get all the medicine Milan and Famagusta can offer. But I know it is in vain. My cancer is terminal. Jana knows nothing as yet. She is coming to see me soon—then I'll tell her the truth. The best I can hope for is extended time.

Now back to Caterina. I too was doing some detective work about her, her commission, her fondness for the present and the picture which might have shown her as a kind of Diana. I was looking for it in the museum's store in Asolo, where she ruled during the last but one phase of her life. Then I searched Campo San Paolo in Venice, I mean in the Cornaro Palace there, and also in my birthplace in Famagusta, where she was queen, and Empress of Armenia as well. The latter was only a titular rank. But now it is late at night, my fountain pen is getting tired, and I'd rather continue this correspondence at another time. Meanwhile, my love to your lovely wife, Helena, she must now be in her seventh or eighth month of pregnancy. Please look after her with continued care, affection and with increasing patience.

Your old friend,

Jirar.

P.S. I am interested in the map. I offer £1,700 for it.

P.P.S. I had written yet not sealed my letter to you when I came upon the correspondence between two Cornaro brothers. Ippolito wrote to Cesare: 'Catherina's horse Pegasus was from our stable at Mestre. It was a grey gelding, fifteen hands tall, with a bushy white mane, fiery eyes, yet mild temper. It had massive legs, like Doric columns, its pasterns were high and hairy, its hoofs enormous. No doubt Caterina felt safe on him, prancing proudly on feast days, cantering, never galloping, in the course of the hunt.' "

7. Caterina

"On 14th February [1489] the queen, dressed in black and accompanied by the barons and their ladies, set off on horseback. Six knights held her horse's reins. From the moment she left Nicosia, her eyes kept streaming with tears. Upon her departure, the whole population was bewailing."

Letter from Caterina Cornaro, Regina di Asolo, to Isabella d'Este Gonzaga, Marchesa di Mantua.

10 December 1509

"Cara Isabella,

I would like to remind you of your promise last year, in Venice, when you assured me of the certainty of your forthcoming visit to Asolo. The dates of our birth are not secret to one another: I am twenty years older than you, and I have been harbouring motherly feelings towards you ever since our first meeting in Ferrara, at the turn of the century. You have been blessed by childbirth and a handsome childbearing figure, a fine taste in arts and firm statesmanship (or should I say: stateswomanship) of the highest calibre. Fate has been good to me at the beginning and cruel later on. My husband, Giacomo II Lusignano, King of Cyprus and Armenia, was a good-looking, and able man (a little vain, an excellent horseman and a gentle husband). It is from him that I learned the love of horses, and we spent many a good time—during the one and only year of our marriage—tending our horses, and leading the hunt. At that time there were fallow deer and plentiful foxes on the island, and hunting was a royal prerogative.

Then my husband died, and later my infant son, in suspicious circumstances. I never remarried. So I spent some of my time visiting the Italian mainland, partly to see my family, especially Andrea Cornaro, my brother, and Marco Bembo, and visited some of the rulers on the eastern coast (Ferrara, Mantua, Rimini) and offered felicitations to their wives.

No one was as *simpatico* to me as your vibrant yet stately and wise self; someone who was ready to sacrifice time and effort for a good-for-nothing husband (excuse my boldness, and sincerity). No one was as dear to my motherly heart as you were.

I first saw you as a princess in your father's stately castle in Ferrara. You were but a girl, studious, and a friend of significant writers, philosophers and notable painters while I was still a Queen of Cyprus. I know I was a willing and obedient pawn in the hands of my family, the Cornaros, leading statesmen of Venice and well-to-do merchants of exceptional diplomatic skills, but—I assure you—I was not ever forced to do anything. I was genuinely fond of Giacomo, and it suited my vanity to be a consort on an exceptionally beautiful island. You know that according to Greek mythology Cyprus was the birthplace of Venus, and, looking at the country lasses of the island in our days, I spot some pale-skinned ones with oriental eyes, some olive-skinned girls with bee stung lips; one must conclude that Cyprus's relative nearness to Europe, Asia and Africa caused an advantageous mixing of blood out of which beauty was born.

Famagusta, in my time, was as well endowed as any Italian city—as Rome, Turin, Florence, and my homeland—Venice, and it was natural that, belonging to the commercial and strategic orbit of Venice, it should eventually be owned by it. The Cypriots did not resent the loss of their sovereignty; this island had always been dominated by one power or another: the Acheans and the Romans in ancient times (when the sanctuary of Aphrodite/Venus was its cultural centre), then by Richard the Lionheart and the Order of Knights, with the Franco-Lusigneurs at their head. With Venice we are still talking about a land mainly populated by Christians. But there is the danger (*minaccia!*), yet few of us would speak plainly about it, that given another heart and shore, the Turks will take it and cover it with their culture and faith and abominable cruelty. You may consult your militaristic husband or His Holiness, the Pope himself, to get convinced of the disunity ruling Italy, nay the Christian world.

Let us enjoy ourselves while we can. I am now *Domina Aceli, signora di Asolo,* I have my court of eighty people and a little army of one hundred soldiers, supplied and maintained by the Venetian Republic. I am now—as reported by Annibale

Crispo, my cousin in Venice—threatened by the likely occupation of the League of Cambrai. I am not really afraid of them: despite their reputation of fierceness, they are all Christians, including your husband.

Before concluding my letter—dictated to Pia Maria of the Minorite Order, and my faithful handmaiden (because at the age of sixty-four I don't see too well any more, for close work)—I want to give a description of a painting by Messer Zorzo of Castelfranco, now in my study.

Andrea Cornaro, my brother, commissioned a portrait of me, on horseback, some time ago. At that point Messer Zorzo was working in Venice, together with the somewhat younger but not less capable Tiziano Vecellio [Titian]. They (or the former) made a sketch, the size of a window in my bedchamber in Venice. There was a hunt at that time around Mestre in which I eagerly took part, and I was dressed accordingly. It took another year or so for Zorzo to enlarge it to life-size and add paint to it profusely, lavishly, half-darkly half-lightly on a canvas. I am in *premier plan*, sitting on a grey charger, with silver tackle, holding the reins with my left hand and wearing a chamois glove, while on my right hand, held high, sits a brown falcon with black beak, talons and eyes. (In truth we didn't use falcons on that occasion.) I am wearing a light brown hunting coat, made of bear skin (it was winter) with large gilded buttons. The horse is animated; it lifts its front right leg and hoof and bows its head, as if nodding. The horsewoman (me) has a face comely and

102

vibrant, and youthful as she was in her forties. My hair, light brown on the portrait, gaily protrudes from under the circular headdress, and it looks as if significantly disarrayed by the prevailing wind which also moves the green leaves of the overhanging bows. The clever and skilful painter sliced twenty years off his model. He might have seen me when a young man (during one of my Venetian visits) or he might have taken his inspiration from my Famagusta portrait, painted in the 1480s. At any rate, the portrait with horse greatly pleases me, I am looking at myself, as I once was, as I saw myself in Famagusta, in the mirror. I see the glinting of my green eyes lit up by the oblique sun rays.

Your long-time friend,
Caterina."

This letter, miscatalogued in the National Archives of Veneto under the name of Pia Maria, with reference to "Santa" Caterina, was discovered—or, more precisely, rediscovered—by me. Caterina's picture has inspired me to consult, then copy, eight lines from *Samson Agonistes*, by Milton.

But who is this, what thing of sea or land?
Female of sex it seems,
That so bedecked, ornate, and gay,
Comes this way sailing,
Like a stately ship . . .
With all her bravery on, and tackle trim,
Sails filled, and streamers waving,
Counted by all the winds that hold them play.

But where did this other life-size painting get to? According to the *Lives of the Artists,* it was, at one time—perhaps in the 1550s—in the possession of "that distinguished gentleman, Giovanni Cornaro". Caterina died in 1510 without an issue. Giovanni was her nephew and one of her heirs.

The historians have a different angle to the Caterina Cornaro story. On the occasion of her marriage, she was given the title of the *"Daughter of St Mark"*, which prompted a Piedmontese bishop to remark that he had never before heard that St Mark had been married, and that, even if he were, he and his wife might not have had a daughter. In a palace coup in Cyprus, both the chamberlain and the doctor of the young queen were assassinated.

The portrait of Caterina—surely the loveliest painting of any queen until Sisi's portrait in the nineteenth century—by Titian, was executed after Caterina's death with the help of an early sketch made at the time of her marriage, possibly by Dürer in 1494–1495. Her portrait by Gentile Bellini, now in the Szépmüvészeti Múzeum in Budapest, is of a later date, possibly 1505. It shows a mature lady, in half profile, with a somewhat chubby but definitely proud and noble demeanour. From under the classical crown of fair hair, a pair of green eyes look out in the distance.

In the torturous fifteenth-century history of Cyprus, the Castanzo family—originally from Sicily—played a leading role. James II of Lusignan had usurped the throne of Cyprus from his stepsister with the help of Muzio Castanzo's fleet, the captain who was later appointed admiral of Cyprus. His son, Tuzio Castanzo (born in Castelfranco), was a general and a trustee in charge of Caterina's military and naval troops. When Cyprus was annexed to Venice, Tuzio entered the service of Venice as a *condottiere* and was named by Louis XII of France as "Italy's premier lance". However, he was never allowed to return to France, and he ended his days in Castelfranco.

Why were the Cypriots so dejected witnessing Caterina leaving the island? She was just, and she was lovely, with a strong character and a soft heart. It was her custom to go to the main square (some called it *piaz*) in Famagusta after Sunday mass and distribute money to the poor. She carried the bronze and silver pieces in her apron, listened to the heartbreaking stories of the poor and distributed alms. She had a very good memory: those who got help one Sunday could not get any more in that given month, unless some disaster had occurred in their life. The alms-giving was repeated in Nicosia as often as in Famagusta.

When I finished translating this sixteenth-century letter into modern English in Milan, looking out through the window of Azirjan's apartment, I saw nothing but the thick fog outside. The faint hooting of a slow bus or a crawling car seeped through my senses. And then, visibly and not too slowly, like someone taking off a macintosh, nature began to divest itself of the urban fog; it lifted, and for ten minutes or so the face of the sun appeared between greyish black clouds. *What a theatre performance*, I thought, because the sky hid again and the clouds gave way slowly, and large flakes of snow began to fall. Falling and flying; there must have been a little waft in the air for some of the snowflakes were dancing in the air, then softly landing, like butterflies, on the top of the buses, cars and on the pavement. It is curious that in my patient searching through Renaissance literature I cannot remember spotting a snowfall in Milan, except in the reverse writing of Leonardo, or was it in Milan? It might have been in France.

The layer of snow that afternoon in Milan was thin, it melted instantly, and the passers-by slipped and skimmed on the slushing surface until they and the whole world outside disappeared in the descending dusk. All but one: one street lamp kept insisting on showing its blurred face.

8. Eve

"Every religion comes from one stem, but the leaves are all different."
(Ienyesseb)

On the eve of Midsummer Night's day, Helena and I were sitting in front of the TV watching Shakespeare's comedy as performed by the English National Theatre company. Then PANG! I thought for a moment that the sound came from the play, perhaps emitted by Titania or Bottom, but no, not at all. I realised that it was Helena who had cried out and almost synchronically grabbed my right arm.

"It is coming," she said, now *sotto voce*, and put my hand on her tummy. Placing a trembling hand on her and feeling the babe's movements was a regular occurrence performed by me, followed regularly by calling the unborn a he or a she, or *Anthony* (a favourite name with me) or *Eve* (Helenka's favourite). Whoever, whichever, we weren't expecting it to come before 10 July, the date given by our doctor as its birth date.

She had had a regular pregnancy with a once a week visit to the gym, a medical examination once a month, which twice involved an ultrasound that, in 1990, could reveal the position of the baby but could not yet show the sex of the unborn child in the womb. Helena had (and has) a comfortable hip, her diet was healthy, and her regular daily walk (except on rainy days)

107

in Bishop's Park maintained her constitution. Around the seventh month or so, she stopped drawing and painting but slowly-slowly redecorated the small room and set up the nursery. Would it be blue or pink? After some mind and heart searching, she painted red poppies on the white wall interspersed with blue violets. I painted the ceiling of every room, bathroom and kitchen included, off-white.

My parents came from time to time. At Easter Helena's mother Maria came with her new husband, Dr Hacha, occupying her old flat in Wimbledon and bringing a handsome soft toy, a bearded dwarf, with her. Our most frequent visitor was Tatyana, Helena's closest friend and my best student. After I discussed her Giorgione project with her, she often closeted herself with Helena and talked of religion. I wasn't intimately interested in the subject: I believe in God but not in the doctrines which I, for the lack of a better thing, willy-nilly go by.

Now, in the middle of Midsummer's Night, and holding on to Helena, I realised that she was all wet below, the thin blanket over us, her pants, my shoes, her thighs. AMBULANCE! The thought hit me really hard, like lightning hitting a dry, unprepared tree in the middle of an unexpected downpour. We had no car, only a bike at that time—sixteen years ago it was—and although Helena on certain days was my occasional pillion passenger, she now required a comfortable vehicle and very fast. I rang the hospital in Hammersmith which was nearest, yet it took them about thirty minutes to arrive. By that time the birth pangs had started, then increased in intensity. Helena lay on a woolly carpet on the floor, a blanket underneath her. I held her right hand. It did not occur to me to prepare towels or hot water or, God forbid, a pair of scissors.

My thoughts raced back and forth. In the ovum, faultlessly fertilised, there is the successfully initiated human being, with its countless possibilities: when it grows up it can be a genius or an idiot, or anything in between. One's senses are like the paddles of a well-designed watermill. Life itself is water—water itself is life. It drives the wheel of the human body, which is three quarters water.

Her spasms increased. "Sponge me down, please, Giorgio," she indicated while opening and closing the fingers on her right hand. I removed her dripping pants and washed her down with warm water. The bell rang. Two hefty ambulance men came with a stretcher, which was not really needed. She walked into the red crossed van. I followed. At the hospital, we were immediately ushered into the labour ward, where an obstetrician and a midwife were waiting for us. He was tall and bald; she was small, rotund, mixed race and smiling. To do something useful, I wiped off the beads of perspiration from Helena's brow.

Then something went awry. The midwife (still smiling) opened up Helena's labia as much as she could with bare hands, and the obstetrician entered her birth canal with a pair of pliers—they were, in fact, forceps. The next few seconds felt like loaded minutes; the medic at length withdrew the instrument. Helena began to cry and give short sharp shrieks, then got an epidural and stopped voicing her pain. Then a cut. The doctor's pate had drops of sweat rolling down his face.

I did not ask permission to be present at the birth of my infant, nor was I given any indication that I shouldn't be. And, untypically, I had never discussed this question with Helena. I never moved my eyes from her. In the pauses of her pangs of spasmodic pain, she breathed regularly, her face was calm, her eyes shone like fireflies. She beckoned with her left hand. I leaned over above her face, and she whispered in my ear: "Giorgio, I feel I am a wine bottle with a cork halfway out but stuck."

I imagined the stretched womb between the hip bones, perhaps as big as an ostrich egg, and a little thing inside there, flapping with arms and feet, making the opening of the neck of the womb increase. The block must have been the head of the infant—that must have been her cork.

"Push," said the midwife.

"Keep pushing," said the doctor.

I could have bellowed there and then but didn't, only covered my eyes. The forceps came out once again. My love only whimpered now. Then came the babe: head, between the forceps, emerging first, then the shoulders, then the rest of her body, arms and legs. She was as red as a poppy but cried with full healthy force, was wiped down, and placed on her mum's breast. Only for a minute. Then she was washed and dried. There was a crown on her head—caused by the forceps—a protuberance that would subside and soon go altogether, said the doctor. Otherwise she was perfectly formed. She had blue eyes (Helena's), wavy black hair (mine) and a perfect nose (unlike my flattened one). After three days mother and child were sent home to Fulham.

Outside the family, Mr Corwen was the first visitor, wearing a raincoat, top hat, waistcoat—it was a Saturday—and bringing a huge bunch of orchids. As the nursery windows were open to the south-east, Helena's eyes were lit up by the oblique Sunday morning sunrays as she glanced at the sight of her flowers.

The babe had already been registered in the hospital as Eve, although this name was only provisional between us until baptism. When my mother and father first visited us, Mum brought up the subject of christening and suggested the Brompton Oratory.

"Francesca," said Helenka to her mother-in-law, "let Eve decide for herself when she wants to be christened, and which faith she wishes to enter."

Shock. My mother sat down on a stool and searched for words. Then, clearing her perspiring face with a tissue, she said: "Helena, dearest. You are a Catholic girl, married in a Catholic church, going to mass on Sundays . . ."

"Yes, before Eve was born and before the scandal at the university. And before Tatyana opened my eyes."

What a bombshell. My dad picked up his granddaughter from her cot and whispered something in her ears.

I muttered, "Helena. What scandal? What university?"

"Yours, Giorgio. Your university class. But you are deaf and blind. You only see the Giorgione reproductions and hear the news about the possible whereabouts of the missing pictures."

"What scandal?" Mamma repeated my question in a quivering voice because, understandably, she was uncommonly upset.

"Imogen was raped by the chaplain."

Hmm. I thought, what curious taste, and what a pervert of a chaplain. The girl is like a beanpole. Good face and good voice and skill in drawing, but as a woman? One might better fancy a stuffed scarecrow than Imogen. And the chaplain? We had no Catholic chaplain. The one attached to the university was a young, quiet Anglican fellow, called Ellis.

"Please explain," I said to Helena, adopting a stern stance, my voice more serious than ever before when addressing her.

"He lives in Florence," she said, then took the baby from her father-in-law and fed her. I thought how nature looks after a mother, physically healthy and with ample motherly instincts. She suckled Eve from her left breast then from her right. The once rose petal breasts were now apple size, and the flowing production of milk was gustily maintained by a daily pint of Guinness. The family conversation about spiritual aspects subsided, giving way to making the baby burp, then changing her nappy. My father had brought her sixty disposable nappies. My mother—"let me, please"—she said, changed a dirty nappy for a clean one. Then Eve went to sleep and we transferred to the living room.

But before that Helena said: "And the priest who raped Imogen was not an isolated case. I too was once attacked by a monk. Luckily I escaped. Giorgio knows about that." She broke down.

Dad stepped over to her and said in his deep basso voice: "*Zitto* (hush), Helena. I only have one son, and one granddaughter. My father was a Catholic, his father too, and his father as well. Not to mention my son, your husband. And you, as far as we know, your family, all the people of your ancestry were all Catholics."

Helena hung her head and clasped her knees. "Yes, almost all of them were Catholics, except one grandmother, my mother's mother. She was Protestant, in fact a proto Hussite."

I persisted: "Please, Helena, explain what happened to Imogen."

"Well, Imogen had corresponded with that chaplain, a kind of expert on Botticelli. They met up in Firenze, looked at all the Botticelli paintings on display there, for two days. On the third day he took her to Fiesole for an outing, food and wine in the basket. He made her drunk. Then at a secluded place he raped her."

Mamma spoke up: "And that is why you do not want my granddaughter to be baptised by the rites of the Catholic Church; do I get it right? Are all priests rapists?"

Helena's eyes filled with tears. "Please do not be angry with me. Faith is a personal thing, and I lost my faith in the teaching of the Roman Catholic Church."

"So, you want her to be like you, do you?" asked my mother, struggling to suppress her anger.

"I want her to be whatever she wants to be. Eventually. And I want her to be like myself. I want to offer my life to Christ," said Helena.

"Why? Don't all the Christians do that irrespective of their denominations or sects?" I asked her, still somewhat incredulously, almost wondering if she were in earnest since she had not informed me of her change of faith or change of mind. We shared a bed, a table and many thoughts.

"Giorgio, I am tired. Eve, lovely though she is, takes a lot out of me. Can I talk about these things again to you another time? I think that your mum and dad are tired too."

"*Annamo a casa*," said Dad, taking the point, and adopting a joking Roman accent. My parents took leave of all of us with kisses and hugs but with a certain stiffness in their body language. The usual caresses of my mother were only meted out to the babe, and Dad's liqueur chocolates stayed in his pocket.

Next Sunday, instead of mass—which I had been frequenting infrequently, although I always attended the main Christian feasts—I went with Helena and Eve to a non-denominational service of the Christian Fellowship. They had hired a hall in the local elementary school, sang songs more than they talked, and ate pieces of white bread, and drank fruit juice for communion.

"They are Bible-based," said Helena, and after the service, the preacher rushed to assure me of the same. "I had always had a problem," Helena said, "in believing in transubstantiation."

"But you had accepted it."

"Yes, but I now confess what I had always suspected, that Christ is not specifically in the host, yet we take the wafer or bread, or whatever, in order to remember him, his sacrifice."

I said to the two of them: "Do you know what Luther thought of Christ's presence in the bread and wine?"

They did not know.

"Luther said that since God was present everywhere, he was present in the host too."

"Should this be the case, the hocus pocus of transubstantiation is totally unnecessary," said she.

The folk attending the service looked genuine, and the Christian order "to love one another" was better kept by them than by any other community I ever knew. As a boy I remember having spent half the time during mass observing the girls, and I wondered how could I keep to the close interpretation of the sixth commandment. I dreaded the confessional. These newly born (reborn) Christians were spilling the beans publicly. Like the Quakers whom I once heard at their service, they stood up and related their spiritual experiences of the past week. The pastor added his comments and handed down his own soul-filling package, which usually involved the conversions of Tom, Dick and Harry.

Not publicly, but after the service privately, I approached the American pastor, a young man with a small crew cut and an earnest expression. "Your new converts, were they all Roman Catholics?"

"Mostly. Those that had been estranged from their

Church or were excluded from taking their sacraments. Divorcees, for instance. But not so long ago we had a Jewish convert too."

Just as he said it I set eyes on a small, black-haired, vibrant girl: Tatyana Corwen. Life is never short of surprises. I think she said, as she approached me, that Giorgione was a person like her, a Hebraic Christian, or an Old Testament Nazarene.

"Well, we don't know that for sure. What we do know is that he fondly dwelt upon Old Testament subjects, like Moses, David, Judith and Holofernes, Samson, Solomon, the three philosophers and perhaps others as well." As I was recounting these names and looking into the bright-burning, coal eyes of my pupil and Helena's best friend, the penny dropped. We were having tea now in the teacher's room behind the class hall where the service had been conducted.

"So it was you who converted Helena?"

Tanya spilt her tea—her hands were shaking. "I can't deny that it was me who called her attention to the fact that we were all sinners, including her."

"But sinners go to confession, don't they?"

"I have not stopped being Jewish even though I have increased and renewed and enriched my faith. The Jews go to the rabbi if something troubles them. My father goes nowhere, to no one; he is an ultra neologue. Well yes, Helena used to go to confession every Easter. But since the scandal with Imogen, she trusts no priest with her inner life."

Without being reborn but not disapproving of her choice, I frequented some of the Sunday services with the Christian Fellowship folk. One Saturday, on someone's birthday, we all went to Hammersmith Arcade and played nine pin bowling. The pastor won. Ruth, the birthday girl, had brought up all her seven living children (three more had died of a congenital ill-ness) and danced in the middle of the floor to Christian tunes. I recognised two of the tunes as being played at more daring Catholic services too. Cool tunes, cool ditties. Helena announced—well, asked—that we should have a "newborn reception party". We did. Most of the community were there, bringing presents, including cakes, puddings, a Babygro, a baby Bible (you can't start too early) and many, many well-wishing cards. Obviously, this was to be the substitute of the baptism we had never had for her.

Mum and Dad did not appear, but Mum had a plan which she communicated to me. Eve had to have her jabs at the clin-ic. I suggested that I should take her, thus letting Helena have a longer sleep after suckling Eve day and night. The clinic was near by, and the medical administration took two minutes. I had wheeled her in her pram to the doctor's. Outside waited Mum and Dad in their car. They gave us a lift—the journey took less than ten minutes—and then a lift back to our home. In between we arranged a private christening ceremony. I pro-nounced the words: "Eve Barbatella, I baptise you in the name of the Father and the Son and the Holy Spirit." Mum held the baby, Dad poured the water on her head, I put oil and salt on her lips and head—and she smiled!

"We have depaganised her," said Dad. "In critical cases, any other Roman Catholic has the right to administer this sacra-ment." I am writing these notes in January 2006. Eve is now a beautiful young lady who—not suspecting her true baptismal state—is preparing for her adult christening in Putney swim-ming pool. After that we shall have a small reception in the hall used normally by girl scouts in Fulham.

Some people have to have dual driving licences. Some

people have dual nationalities. Some people have dual baptisms because their parents differ in matters of faith. (Two is better than none.)

9. London

*"It may be more interesting to stay in London than to dwell in
Heaven because there may be more streets in London than
mansions in the sky."*
(*The Chronicle of London*)

Eve's first birthday was celebrated on the otherwise empty
stage of the park theatre in the middle of Bishop's Park, half
circled by blooming flower beds, where the blossoms were fragile and motionless, and half surrounded by the escarpment of a
carefully manicured lawn. She enjoyed feeding the seagulls with
pieces of half-eaten sandwiches and morsels of birthday cake.
Then she sat back comfortably into her pushchair, and there
uttered her first, almost complete sentence on spotting a running dog: "Look at that bow-wow! Good bye!"

We all cheered, perhaps even more than necessary. At the
point of finishing the "Happy Birthday to You" the sun shone
with unusual brightness and strength, although it was already
afternoon and the dark shadows began to stretch. The birthday
party consisted of Shirley, another little girl of Eve's age living
in our neighbourhood, Maria, who had come back from Prague
just for her granddaughter's birthday, bringing with her an enormous stuffed dog bigger than Eve, and Mr and Mrs Corwen,
my parents and us.

Jana Blindalova did not come. Jirar Azirjan was poorly so she had left Genoa and moved in with him in Milan.

In an unobserved minute, Mamma gently pulled me to the side and whispered in my ear, "I am so glad we've managed to baptise her, because, God forbid, she might any day contract an incurable illness, and and . . . and without having received this vital sacrament she might land in limbo."

Mum could not have foreseen that Pope Benedict would do away with the concept of limbo in 2006.

> *The story told by Pliny credits the invention of painting to the daughter of a potter of Sicyon. Her love being about to go on a long journey, she traced the outline of her lover's shadow cast on the wall. This legend claims that the birth of visual arts was provoked by the desire to recall the image of the loved one. The motion of the mind moves with simple actions and ease, since the object of the motion is in the mind, which does not move the senses occupied within itself . . . the hands, and the arms should demonstrate the intention of their mover since those who have vivid emotions accompany all intentions of their minds with vivid movements.*
>
> *This observation should be extended to the movement of leaps, the postures of the body, the positioning of the dominant figures and actions, and the contrasting emphasis expressed by the use of colours.*

This is the start of Tatyana Corwin's BA thesis on Giorgione, the painter. She then continues with the analysis of *The Adoration of the Kings,* a small oil painting on wood, now in the National Gallery in London. One Sunday afternoon, the three of us, Helena, Eve and I, went to the National Gallery, partly to inspect this painting, partly to see the sunset, *Il Tramonto* and another Giorgione landscape which is also kept there. As regards the sunset, we were unsuccessful: the painting had been sent to the restoration lab to fix a few pigments of maroon and to give it a general cleaning. But the kings were there, relatively fresh from a relatively recent light-cleaning job. The blue blouses of Joseph and Mary and the red doublet of one of the servants shone brightly in the afternoon sunshine.

> The ultramarines do not, necessarily, dominate in the colour scheme [wrote my pupil], because the reds (possibly madder) counter balance the blues, and the gold (manifested by St Joseph's cape) gives a focal point to the painting. There is light blue on the top corner of the gift presentation scene, which is the sky; a patch of very showy off-white being the trousers of one of the servants, maroon and dark brown emphasising the background. Small as the picture is, and presumably originally (one foot by three) decorating a *predella*, it lacks the accepted Giorgionesque feature: impressive figures against an expressive landscape. We have no landscape at all here, and the gift offered (gold) is not to the child or to Mary but to St Joseph, normally a humble stepfather; but here he is a central, almost a dominating, princely figure. It is not unusual for Renaissance painters that they dress the Holy Family in festive garments.

Giorgione follows suit, ignoring the tradition of the tight-lipped Bible, which suggests that Jesus' parents were rather poor people. Well, if they had been poor before the visit of the three wise men, Casper, Melchior and Balthazar (who is as dark on this picture as tradition suggests), the gifts of gold, frankincense and myrrh made them at least people of medium means, even if they were giving away the myrrh and frankincense to the temple in Jerusalem. I would guess that the gold was financing their journey and stay in Egypt carried out to avoid the rage of Herod.

It is not impossible—but not too likely either—that the picture with the three Magi and the elevated figure of St Joseph is from the same hand as were the minuscule figures in the Gonzaga *Book of Hours. Lege artio.*

Tanya in her thesis accepted the dating of the three Magi as 1506, and the material basis of this picture is cedar wood. Moving chronologically—or as near to that as possible—Tatyana Corwen tackled the *Painting of a Young Woman,* usually named as Laura, which is kept in the Gemäldegalerie of the Viennese Kunsthistorisches Museum.

She now quoted a bit about the technique and the condition of this painting, thanks to Enke Oberthaler's essay in Sylvia Ferino-Pagden's book, *Giorgione* (Vienna, 2004):

"The originally rectangular picture has now an oval shape due to the eighteenth century restoration; what we now have is a canvas fixed on to spruce wood, its edges scalloped. The young woman of the painting has her flesh painted with an amount of lead white. The shadows are resolved with brown glazings. Laura's red coat consists of a bright under painting, warmer in tone with glazes of organic red lake."

The essayist finds it remarkable that the background laurel leaves show fine lines in various shades of green placed next to one another, because this graphical handling brings to mind Leonardo's portrait of *Ginevra da'Benci.* The landscape behind

Laura is also somewhat similar to the landscape behind Ginevra (now *pentimento*); this makes the proposition that Giorgione was interested in Leonardo's technique quite likely.

Laura is a lovely young girl in a sensuous position: the red nipple of her right breast comes out from the fine muslin shawl which is framed by a wide ermine collar of a red gown. Her deep brown hair is plaited on top; one lock drapes down by her full neck, touching her left shoulder. On her regular, round, reddish face the most dominant features are her full bursting lips, her nose, which has a Roman cut, and her brown eyes, which radiate strength, determination and (perhaps) sex appeal. The acanthus leaves around her figure give a festive atmosphere to this semi-profile portrait.

"At a guess, I would say she was twenty years old, a titchy bit younger, and far more attractive and fleshy than myself."

Our vital information comes again from Vasari: *Aveva veduto il Giorgione alcune cose di Leonardo motto fumeggiate e cacciate, come si e detto, terribilmente di scuro: e questa maniera gli piacque tanto, che mentre visse, sempre andó dietro a quella.* (We have seen that Giorgione in Leonardo's manner 'fumigated' [darkened the complete painting], making it very dark; and in this manner he painted much always going back to it.")

The portrait inspired Chlorio to write a poem in Latin called *Giorgione's Laura:*

> My friend and companion, Laura
> You make good poetry with meter and rhythm
> And play merrily on the fine zither
> In our home, in Arcady.
> Giorgione, you paint beauty
> With art, and great pleasure.
> The breast is reflected on board

Your pencil knows its measure.
(translated by Giorgio Barbatella)

We know from a document concerning Vincenzo Catena that this picture was finished in June 1506, at the time when renovations began on the Fondaco Tedeschi. But we don't know (yet?) who Laura was, and who commissioned *messere* Zorzo to paint her. There are many versions or copies of *Laura*, none of them resembling her namesake, the lover of Petrarch, blue-eyed, blonde lady that she was. The laurel leaves allude to Daphne, who metamorphosed into a laurel tree in order to avoid the advances of Apollo, but her brazen exposition of the breast suggests that she may have been a courtesan. Her fur-lined red garment may be the winter dress of Venetian women of pleasure. Whatever she was or wasn't, she is oozing eroticism—as much as Giorgione's *Venus* (perhaps a counterpart) or any of Titian's naked women do.

Although Tatyana had successfully completed her BA thesis, she was not satisfied with the knowledge gained and displayed by her about Giorgione, so she boarded a plane to Dresden to execute further research and accumulate experience with the view to an eventual journey to Castelfranco.

Helena, who had little spare time before the birth of Eve and during her infancy, had since decided to discover London with her daughter. They visited the zoo on two occasions, back to back, explored Regent's Park, not for any sights there, but gazing at the merry-go-round, the dodgem cars, the target shooters, the roller coaster. Returning late in the afternoon and forgetting about her own supper and mine—Eve had her baby food—Helena said: "Life is like a roller coaster, once up, once down."

"Hmm. Life could be like an avalanche, once down, never up."

Her beautiful eyes filled with tears.

I continued: "Oh yes, one day we will eventually die. But we have continuation: Eve. When she grows up she will get married and produce our grandchildren. And they will act likewise."

"We may not all die." (Her eyes had dried up.) "The end is nigh. If it came in our lifetime—I mean the end of the world—we would experience the birth of a new world, alive."

"The logic is faultless. But where did you get the idea that the end of this world was near?"

"The pastor's teaching. He was interpreting Revelation."

I brought the Bible. (It was getting late in the evening; Eve was already asleep in her cot.) "St John says—I suppose the same John whom Jesus loved—at the end of his apocalyptic story, that 'these things will come to pass soon'."

"So you see! Soon."

"But not soon enough. Revelation was written about 1900 odd years ago, and we are still around."

On one occasion mother and daughter were visiting Kew Gardens. Cooked supper was once again omitted, but I had Milano salami at home and ciabatta, so we did not go to bed hungry.

In bed, snuggling, resting her head in the crook of my arm, Helena murmured: "We spent hours gazing at the *rafflesia arnoldii,* the world's greatest flower. It had a scent so penetrating that it could put you to sleep. Eve was asleep, I had had a strong coffee. The size of this flower is about four feet across. The smell comes from the chalice, which is as red as the dawn. I was witnessing the last stages of the flower's bloom. It started slowly to wither. The chalice was slowly turning pink, and the giant petals were losing their fullness. We witnessed the flower's agony but came away before it died."

"The petals fall, life gallops away."

"Yes. I imagined that if I had stayed on any longer there, I would have shrunk and finally fallen like the petals."

"You imagine a lot of things."

"I do. Images run through my mind like pictures in a movie. And then I often home in on a movie clip and sail away."

"Why don't you take up the brush again?"

"That is why. The pictures are tumultuous in my own eye, they don't stay long enough at any one place, and at one point I run away with each and every one. In the zoo I imagined that a giant pelican took me in her beak and carried me away to Arcadia. Looking at the waves of the Thames in Bishop's Park, I imagined a tsunami, a giant surge of floodwater, caused by earth tremors, that took Eve in her pushchair and swallowed her up."

"When I present Eve's dinner, I imagine you at the university, eating your lunch, swallowing a poisonous mushroom and curling up as a wax figure in a glass case, next to Jeremy Bentham."

"Don't you ever daydream of pleasant things?"

"Yes, I do. Not too often. I picture Jirar Azirjan being recovered to perfect health. We go down in his Mercedes to Rome, where I have never been, and visit the Galleria Borghese. There I see Daphnis and Chloe, as sculpted in marble by Bernini, with the girl turning to acanthus leaves to avoid his unwanted attention. I am her leaves and all."

"The frustrated hero of the original myth was Apollo. I hope I am not identified with him in your daydream. I am not as handsome."

"No, you are not. When you appear, you stay. You are the only constant thing in my imagination. You are St George. I am the maiden, the dragon's prisoner. I am waiting for you to slay the dragon."

That became my almost daily occupation, i.e. my night-time occupation: slaying her dragons. Almost, I said, because sometimes she stayed on in the living room, looking at one late TV programme or another, munching her biscuits and drinking cups of tea. Sometimes the tea was changed for sweet wine or amaretto liqueur. The bedroom then, and later lingeringly, pleasantly smelt of alcohol.

There was a deranged young man roaming our streets in Fulham who once cornered Helena and Eve. I was coming home from the university at sunset and saw them talking in front of our semi (bought on a twenty-five year mortgage). He had filthy hair, dirty clothing, and was flailing his arms as he spoke. She stood there like a pillar of salt. When he saw me approaching he ran away.

"He is all alone," said Helena. "His parents turfed him out of his home. He set fire to their shed."

"I beg you: leave him to his own devices. He might set fire to his own hair and your birdhouses. Have you not observed that the sparrows and starlings, usually gathering up at our willow tree and up above on the electric wires, have all moved on, fearing his presence?"

This was a successful argument of mine. *Birds after all.* .

As the months and the years went by, Eve began to assume a distinct personality. She unmistakably showed two different traits: she could be excited, running to and fro, moving from corner to corner as if searching for something. At other times she played with dolls and stuffed animals, intermittently; her

favourite was *Cane,* a fluffy cocker spaniel with a rubber face
and two large brown eyes. It was her constant companion in
bed; without Cane she would hardly ever go to sleep. Although
her native language was English—and soon she spoke with a
Cockney accent due to her mixing, twice a week, with other
toddlers in the nursery school—she also had a vocabulary of
Czech words and Italian expressions. Helena and I normally
spoke in English to one another but—when she was upset or
extra emotional—she lapsed into Italian, her adoptive mother
tongue. So Eve would occasionally exclaim: "*a che dice*" (who
are you telling) or say "*benissimo*" (very well) or even "*tutto in
ordine*" (all is well)—thus settling an argument between her parents. This was always successful: whatever our former disagreement, we echoed her "*tutto in ordine*" and kissed one another
triangularly.

Eve was a girl with a variety of temperaments. She was able
to occupy herself for a longish time as she doodled, messed with
her mother's paints or played with her dog, but she was quick
to anger when denied something she badly wanted. Reluctantly
she let the neighbour's girl play with Cane for a while. Then
she demanded it back, saying it was the toy dog's feeding time.
Its favourite food was Smarties, and a paper bag filled with it
was already in Eve's hand. When the dog wasn't handed over
on demand, Eve smashed the bag of Smarties on her friend's
head. Shirley cried inconsolably.

I am keen on swimming, and I wanted to teach the skill
to Eve early on. It took me a year of going to Putney swimming pool on chosen free Saturdays to make her at least buoy-
ant in the water. She enjoyed swimming, but her strokes were
irregular, and she couldn't harmonise her hand movements,
the arm pull, with the frog-kick of her legs. Helena came with

us relatively rarely, she preferred the waves of the sea to chlorine-filled, swimming-pool water.

Eve was not always a fast moving child, indeed she could be ponderous, but she possessed a dynamism which made me think she could be a fencer one day. My uncle, the fencing master Giuseppe della Croce, visited us again one day—his team once again was fencing against an English team—and taught Eve a game called "red paws". One of the two participants has to cover with two hands the opponent's palms. The hands underneath endeavour to move up above quickly and slap the covering hands. Soon Eve, at the age of four, often got the better of both her parents. She liked walking; we made weekend trips to Oxford, and there we walked on Box Hill; Sunday journeys to Hampstead; to Greenwich, and to Henley, where we hired a rowing boat and crossed the Thames three times to and fro. Once we went as far as Brighton: this was the virgin voyage of my seven-year-old Ford. The weather was inclement, a strong wind slapping up biggish waves; Eve spent most of her time riding on my neck.

"No pwoblem, Dad," she giggled.

In 1996, ten years ago, my father won £10,000 on the pools. He gave me £5,000 to lessen our mortgage burden and begged my mother to let him spend the rest as he wished. She consented. They were reasonably well off—Dad was still setting up and maintaining private gardens—so why shouldn't he, for the first time in his life, splash out the way he wished? Being a landlubber from Castelfranco, but spending the bulk of his adult life next to Father Thames, it was not, perhaps, totally surprising that he wished to conduct a river journey with those closest to him: his family. The launch, hired at Hampton Court for the day, could carry twenty people under a tarpaulin. Dad had taken a couple of lessons in operating and navigating it.

And the crew? Mum and Dad, Ricardo of the La Bocca, Agostino Belli and his wife Emma, my parents' friends, us three, Helena, Eve and me, then Shirley, Eve's friend, with her parents, and finally two clerics: the nondenominational pastor and Chaplain King, lately appointed to a vacant post in Brompton Oratory.

Although invited, and expected, Helena's mother could not come: she had just sprained her ankle.

The morning was resplendent, no wind, not even a breeze to comb the sheen of the river, brightest sunshine sparkling on the bridges, under which we chugged along, with ice-cream in an icebox for the kids. There were three more children all over ten, the children of the chaplain.

I was expecting intellectual sparks bursting forth from the mouths of the two men of God representing two different shades of Christianity—"by faith alone" and "good works, good faith"—but they peacefully leaned on the guard of the launch and talked about cooking. Chaplain King was a widower, his wife had died some years ago, and his children were being brought up with the help of his sister. The pastor was a keen angler who, apart from catching the fish deftly, was also cooking it passionately.

I had fitted the two six-year-old girls, Shirley and Eve, with swimming armbands. Though both of them could swim, they were both very lively, and with their running up and down on the deck they presented a "liability" (Mum's word).

I settled down on a bench near the steering wheel, operated by the steersmen (Dad and helped by the steers mate, Agostino). The two middle-aged ladies, Mum and Emma (who, incidentally, was English, so the groups had to chatter in Chaucer's language), were opening the other icebox, containing orange juice, and pouring out paper cupfuls for all those who had queued for it.

At one point Dad said: "Giorgio, take the wheel; beware of other boats and the silver pillars of the bridges—go between them, not against them." So I took the wheel and the two old stagers began to sing. First it was the "*Fanciulla fanciulla, tu sei bella . . .*", then "*Dolce far Niente*", then two arias from "*Il barbiere di Siviglia*" and then the entrance song of the *Principessa* from the "*Principessa di Czardas*". We were already under the central arch of Hammersmith Bridge in west London, perhaps the most elegant of the Thames bridges, constructed by Adam Clarke.

Emma was not a run of the mill woman. She wore a Girardi sunhat, an apron decorated with tulips and a large emerald ring on her left hand. Agostino had found the emerald. From the wafts of her alto voice I gathered interesting information. Her father had been a bridge maintenance man, working on almost all the London Thames bridges: Albert, Chelsea, Vauxhall, giving them a fresh coat of paint (as part of a team) once every ten years. He had oiled the traverses of Lambeth, the pillars of Westminster Bridge—we were to sail under them—used air brush on Blackfriars Bridge, pug mill, paint sprayer and doge sludge on and under Tower Bridge. Although he had stopped painting some twenty years before, the old codger was still around and healthy at ninety-three.

Dad's voice was deep basso, while Agostino emitted sounds of a baritone-tenor. Ricardo, who had no singing voice at all, hummed and hawed rhythmically.

The two men of God were staying in the middle of the

boat, where the footbridge was also stored; the golden oldies stayed in the front of the boat, behind me, and the children were here and there and everywhere. Helena sat in the back of the launch gazing at the eddies and whirlpools caused by the propeller.

I handed the wheel to Agostino, a very strong, muscular, burly man, who hailed from Veneto and had spent most of his working life in London as a stonecutter. I joined my wife, sitting down next to her on the bench. Her face was wet, due to— I thought—the rising vapour of the river as the water was being cut up by the launch. But no, she was crying . . .

"What's wrong?"

"Everything. The world will end. We shall not see Eve growing up. You will never finish your book on Giorgione, and I will not paint another picture."

"Of course you will. And the world will not end all that soon. The approaching second millennium plants these thoughts of world-ending into the mind of your pastors. And they are keen to trumpet them into yours."

"Giorgio! You forget the prophesies of St John in Revelation. All the signs are around us now."

"I know: the Antichrist. There were two already in this century, called Hitler and Stalin, but the world has survived them."

"OK. But what about the nuclear catastrophe, looming large by the stockpile of nukes? And what about those wicked, giant asteroids? One collision and we are finished."

"These are unlikely scenarios. Embrace me and kiss me; today's celebration is also your birthday feast as well as my elders' wedding anniversary."

She embraced and kissed me. She had increased her weight since childbirth by a stone and a half. This made it a necessity to renew her wardrobe at least once a year. I had not changed bodywise: I was thirteen stone then, in 1996, and I am the same size now in 2006.

We docked at Chelsea Bridge. Not at the nearest pillar but a couple of hundred yards downriver in the vicinity of the houseboats. And there a small miracle was taking place. The vessel called *Bocca* opened, and two waiters began to transfer dishes of delicious nosh to our boat, balancing the trays in one hand and holding the rail of the footbridge with the other. We had oysters on ice, caviar, herring, *vitello tonato*, fried red peppers, *calamari*, fresh *ciabatta*, then *panettone* with wine sauce, and liqueur. Ricardo gave the toast. "I wish to celebrate the wedding anniversary of my good friends, Francesca and Giorgio seniore, as well as the birthday of their lovely daughter-in-law: Helena!"

She had cheered up, clinked her glass with the others; the wine was one single portion of Chianti *bolla*. "A river journey," said Ricardo, "commands temperance."

When all was said and eaten we pushed on to Westminster, the furthest station from our start, turned around (the turn neatly done by Dad) and sailed (chugged) downriver.

Once again we docked under Chelsea Bridge. Once again the *Bocca* opened wide. A trolley was pushed out and a two-storey giant celebration cake was transferred to our boat. The top layer was a white creamy Russian cream *torta*, a favourite with the Slavs; the bottom layer was a chocolate "tree trunk cake", a speciality of the patisserie under the Rialto Bridge in Venice. Ricardo was once an apprentice there. The children had an ice-cream once more.

Eve had a doll, called Daisie, who was also fed with a variety of sweets and puddings. Then I noticed from afar that Daisie was having a bath in the Thames, lowered by Eve on a ribbon that she had untied from her hair. Just as I was making a move to intervene, I saw with horror Eve, in an effort to submerge her doll, keel over the guard and splash into the Thames. This splash was immediately followed by another. Father King, the Catholic chaplain, jumped after my girl, grabbed her by her long loose hair and scrambled over with her to the dock of the houseboat *Bocca*. (In his civilian life he was once a swimming instructor and a trained lifeguard.) When Helena realised what had happened—she had followed me to the middle of the launch—she collapsed and fainted. Eve, wet but cheerful, woke her mother up with hugs and kisses.

As we docked peacefully and filed out of the launch in orderly fashion, fluffs descending from the sky, looking like weightless, warm snowflakes; and before we left our station at Hampton, a head emerged from mid-river blowing jets of air vapour—a bottlenose whale was visiting the Thames (coming from Norway or even further North). We gazed and gaped at it, as it swam, bellowing, sprinkling sprays of water, then we departed.

"Leviathan," said Helena with glee, and tugged at my shirt.

10. Tempora Mutantur

"The poor beatle, which we tread upon
In corporal sufferance finds a pang as great
As when a girl dies."
(Shakespeare: modified)

"Hullo!"

"Hullo."

"Is that you, Giorgio?"

"It is me, Jirar. I recognise your unmistakable voice."

"You mean croaking, don't you?"

"I mean your baritone with a touch of heavy shade. Hoar frost on the voice."

"Not for long, not for long any more. I have been doing the diet of Miss Bishop's as described in her book: *It Is Time to Heal.* It has prolonged my life, but now only months or weeks are left for me in the valley of shadows."

"How do you know? Has the cancer spread?"

"It had been contained for years but now has come back with a vengeance."

"Where to?"

"The bones are attacked, all over. Both legs, the hips, I can no longer walk. I am sitting in a wheelchair, and Jana is wheeling me about. I'll leave the flat for her. She is now ensconced in

134

Milan. She teaches violin there. She might sell her Genoa flat and keep the nest egg in the bank. I have made my will; I'll send you a copy. The contents of my apartment will be distributed amongst friends and relatives. Jana will want to have her own things and will migrate from Genoa to Milan. Maria and Dr Hacha will have my desk, and you, two painters, will inherit the Venice canalscape painted by Longhi."

"But, Jirar, that might be worth a couple of million. Are you sure?" (My heart leapt and I became so excited over that, for a second or two I was searching for air.) *Il Canale Grande con Gondole.*

"Ho, ho, ho . . ." (small croaky laughter). "There is plenty more to go to my relatives, especially to David Azirjan, my nephew. He is an antiquarian bookseller and lives in Rome. He'll have the contents of the Milan shop too. He can now branch out beyond antiquarian books to selling antiques under the same auspices that I was selling my stuff. Half of the profit must go to Famagusta, to the Armenian Hospital. By the way, I want to be buried in the Armenian cemetery in Cyprus. I made Jana swear that I will get a proper Armenian Catholic burial—no cremation. One has to think of the last day: God and his angels will have an easier task assembling the molecules of bone-dust (the disease will have gone out of it by that time) than reassembling the atoms of scattered ashes. So, well, are you OK, Giorgio?"

"Reasonably so. Eve is doing very well in elementary school, Helena has no physical complaints . . ."

"But non-physical?"

"I'd rather not talk about that on the telephone. We might just go over to you in the Christmas vac."

"Hmm. The Christmas vac. It is now October. I might just

celebrate another of Christ's birthdays in his birthplace: planet earth. I am rather tired now, but don't you put down the receiver, someone else wants to talk to you, as well."

"Hello."

"I recognise your voice although I have not heard from you for a year or more."

"Mr Barbatella . . . I mean Giorgio. A lot has been happening . . ."

"I hope mostly positive, Tatyana."

"We shall have to wait and see."

"Anyway, you collected your MA two years ago, that being the comparison between *Judith* and *Sleeping Venus,* both by Giorgione da Castelfranco."

"Yes, true. But you may remember that I cast doubt on the title of *Sleeping Venus*. To me she is/was rather daydreaming than sleeping. A sleeping position, physiologically, would hardly (or at any rate very rarely) allow for the crossing of the legs one calf upon the other. The sleeper would straighten her legs. By the way, the Dresden painting is in the best condition of all the Zorzo paintings I have seen."

"And you have seen a lot, including *Judith* in the Hermitage."

"Yes. And we are talking of the same woman, the same model, remember? I am not saying, of course, that she (whoever she was) was the only model he used. Take the woman in *La Tempesta,* or the *Allegory of Chastity* in Amsterdam. 'The more the merrier,' Giorgione was reported saying. And, 'none tells the truth.' I grant you the similarities of *Judith* and *Venus* but if so, why don't the authorities pronounce on it?"

"I give you one reason," I said. "The identification game since Berenson, and indeed Morelli before him, was mostly based on the comparisons of hands and ears. The crown of hair of Venus, and that of Judith, prevents us from seeing the ears, and both of the two women only allow us to see their left hands. In the case of Judith, it rests on her dress, while Venus covers her pudenda with it. Yet they are the same, I mean painted by the same artist who also painted the two exquisite left legs and feet."

"Another indication is the verisimilitude of the greenery. The same type of bushes, the same type of trees. The presence of evergreens, or one of them. Giorgione seemed to place a eucalyptus tree (or a poplar?) in the centre of his background."

"You are quite convincing. But we still have no idea who the model was, have we?"

"I have an inkling, but with the subject selected for my PhD you put me off the close examination track and opened the whole field for me."

"Doctoral theses are not dogma. You may remember mine: 'From Background to Foreground: the Use of Nature in Renaissance Painting' was my first title. I cast my net too wide; the final draught was entitled: '*Et in Arcadia, ego:* Giorgione's use of nature'. Then even that was changed, actually by Helena, a more poetic soul, into: 'Nature, as the Architecture of the Soul'. So what can you say? You have not informed us of your progress, have you?"

"Well. How should I say it? My progress has been thwarted by new developments. My task was to map up all the paintings attributed to Giorgione including those where he might just have had a hand and those which are doubtful, either being copies or the works of his followers."

"Yes," I agreed. "This was to tie in with my own work on the Renaissance Circle, the subject of my own research. A set of comparisons between the paintings of Giorgione, Vincenzo Cartena, Palma Vecchio, Tiziano, Dosso Dossi and Sebastiano del Piombo."

"Sebastiano of the Lead or the Tin. The only one who painted consistently brunettes, women resembling me . . ."

"Perhaps not as lively as you. But let's go back to your PhD topic."

"If you insist. My dad, as you know, is not a poor man, and not insensitive to art, so I got a generous endowment from him on top of my grant from London University. First I went to the Rijksmuseum in Amsterdam to see *Allegoria della Castità*, then to Berlin for *Cerere*, and the *Ritratto di giovane uomo* both in the Staatliche Museum Gemäldegalerie-Dahlem. I came back to Britain, and in Bowood, Wiltshire, I saw *Pastore con Flauto* in the collection of the Marquis of Landsdown. After that I visited Castle Howard, in Yorkshire, to have an extended look at the collection of the Marchese di Northampton which includes *Paedaggio con Giovane Madre e Alabardiere*."

"And even more?"

"In Hampton Court I saw the *Bust of a Young Woman*, and *Concerto*; I re-examined *The Adoration of the Magi*, *The Homage of a Poet* and the *Stories of Damone and Tirsi* in the National Museum; and on Jirar Azirjan's behest I obtained a photo of the *Ritratto di antiquario*. Then, exploring Milan with a guide recommended by Azirjan, I saw *Samsone Deriso* in the Collezione di Mattioli, *Ritorno di Giuditta*, a new discovery for me in Collezione Resini, and *Ragazzo* in the Ambrosiana."

"Your survey is perhaps unprecedented."

"That's what I'd thought. *Venere Dormiente* in Dresden was an old friend. In Florence I spent a fortnight surveying *Cavaliere di Malta*, *Giudizio di Salamone* and *Guerriero con Scuderio*, *Mosé alla Prova del Fuoco*, *Flora*, and a disegno entitled *Agglomerato ai bordi di un fiume*, all in the Uffizi. *Il Concerto* and *Le Tré Étà delle'Uomo* in the Galleria Palatino di Palazzo Pitti. I was about to purchase a plane ticket to the States when the disaster struck . . ."

"Work related or health related?"

"Hmm. Both. You could say a negative double whammy hit me, as if I were under the fork lightning of *The Tempest*."

"And are you all right now?"

"I am not worse, and I have found a considerate and thorough Turkish doctor who treats me."

"May I ask about the nature of your ill health?"

"Excuse me. You may not: it is private. If I am cured, I'll probably tell you what it was."

"Then this mysterious illness has stopped you continuing with your doctorate?"

"No. This was just one thing which had dogged me all my adult life, and got progressively worse. What stopped me in my work was the discovery of the Museo Giorgione."

"I've never heard of it."

"It does not exist in reality, only on paper and in cyberspace. It is a project that was initiated in Castelfranco Veneto by an art historian called Angelo Miatello. He has mapped up the whole Giorgione and Giorgionesque territory. Much of it is described—although not in detail—on the internet."

"Don't lose heart. You have not yet been to Rome. You have not seen the two Giorgione paintings, *The Passionate Singer* and *The Flute Player*, in the Galleria Borghese. I have not seen these either. Perhaps the *Suonatore di Flauto* is not even in the Borghese, but in the Spada. And then, the *Doppio Ritratto* must also be inspected in the Museo di Palazzo Venezia. Unique. We could easily transform the subject of your PhD focusing on the 'Rome paintings of Giorgione'. How about that topic and penumbra? Plenty of mysteries surrounding them to be discovered or at least to weigh up the probabilities.

"Who was the *Cantore*; by whom and where was he painted? According to the dean of the cathedral of St Mark, Venice, there is a list of soloists, extant, between 1400–1900. Was he one of them? The dress and headdress of the singer shows a young man from Lombardy rather than from Venice. The feather in the cap conjures up the origin of the pages at the court of the Visconti. Although we cannot *hear* only *see* the singing— the open mouth, the change of the colouring in his cheeks, the rosy tint, all suggest a *tenor* singing a high note. *The Flute Player* (a companion picture) could easily be a youth performing together with the singer. He could not have been singing in the church as he wears his hat. He might have been singing a madrigal in open air, and the occasion might have been the festivities accompanying the launching of the *Bucefalo* with the Doge on board, carrying the wedding ring which he was going to toss in the water to wed Venice to the Mediterranean sea . . . Which brings me to the point of another puzzle: why didn't Giorgione paint seamen with seascapes as background?"

"I can't say. Not yet. First I'd like to get better acquainted with them before embarking on a new theme."

"That was a long phone conversation. A marathon. Do you have any message for Helena?"

"I would have, but I'd rather talk to her personally and directly. I'll phone her to make arrangements."

"*Addio*, Tanya."

"*Addio*."

We spent Christmas in Milan with Jana, Maria and Dr Hacha, visiting from Prague, and met up with Tanya too. When we arrived in Malpensa there was a thick layer of fog on the ground of the airport and patches of snow. Eve made snowballs, took them and began to bombard the passengers descending the ladder. In town the fog got thicker. "The houses have their blankets on," she said. Next day it cleared, and the night was bright with stars doing their best to outshine the street lights. Eve picked out Cassiopeia, the Big Wheel and the Polar star. Tanya was in Ospedale di Santo Spirito on a hormonal course for four weeks, as ordered and conducted by Dr Ibrahim Pamuk. Mr Corwen came too to see his daughter in the hospital, then returned to London. He had arranged the transfer of *Canale Grande* by Longhi from Milan to our semi in Fulham.

Jirar Azirjan did not wait for Christmas or to receive us: he passed away on 7 November, which would have been the eightieth anniversary of the glorious Soviet Revolution. I have heard about a prophecy, proclaimed by the two young witnesses of Lourdes, that Christianity was to return to Russia in the late Eighties. We had missed Jirar's funeral, which was arranged by Jana according to the antique dealer's instructions, and she was duly assisted by Jirar's nephew, David Azirjan, of Rome. He looked after his uncle's worldly possessions; most of them went to him, anyway, but, apart from letting me have the Longhi, he also passed on to me an envelope with my name on it in the handwriting of Jirar Azirjan. He wrote:

> "A noble ancestor of mine, named Armenius, in Renaissance fashion, was the first Azirjan of note. According to tradition, the family had hailed from Yerevan, but late in the fifteenth century a branch of the family emigrated to Famagusta in Cyprus and

stayed there, under the Lusignan king and his wife. The Azirjans were prosperous merchants dealing in olives, spices, olive oil and wine. At one point at the end of that century, the most learned and distinguished son of the family, the above named Armenius, transferred to Rome and practised medicine there. He was married with two children, and we have no record of his death or burial, be it in Rome or back in Cyprus. I have (or rather *had*) a letter or a memorial script which was written in Armenian but, alas, I have mislaid—misplaced this document. The shop has several thousand items in it—a portion of which is uncatalogued—so there is hope that Armenius' testimony might surface one day. If it does, the document should be handed over to Dr Giorgio Barbatella, that is you, to boost his studies on the Italian Renaissance."

Well, the Armenius document had not turned up (yet), but I had not given up hope that one day it would. David Azirjan had at least six large boxes of uncatalogued documents, and unregistered antique or second hand objects in his transit van.

Leaving Eve with her grandmother, Helena and I went to the hospital to see Tanya. She was in a private room, resting, under the strict instruction of Dr Pamuk to move *no more,* daily, than to go to the toilet. She was cheerful, her cheeks rosy, her black hair forming a crown on the top of her head, à la Venus or Judith. Although she was still shy about her condition and reluctant to enlighten us, her doctor was quite frank about it.

I was present when he approached Mr Corwen. The Harrods manager, impeccably dressed as always, seemed pretty uncomfortable at this encounter, shifting his weight from one leg to the other. The Turk wore a white medical coat, spats on his feet and two-tone shoes. He spoke good English in a somewhat exaggerated accent, stressing his vowels more than necessary.

"I think your daughter is on the mend."

Mr Corwen cleared his throat: "If so, I'll be ever so grateful to you. She has had this menstrual problem ever since she was a teenager."

"Yes, indeed. She could not maintain a proper menstrual cycle; two weeks, three weeks, and she bled, losing the premature egg in the process."

"So she could never have conceived, could she? We had consulted famous doctors in Harley Street, they stuffed her with medicines which produced no results."

"This condition of very irregular menstruation which does not let the egg mature is also very painful and does not normally improve with age."

"My daughter is not yet forty."

"I know. She has been suffering with menorrhagia: in other words, excessive bleeding which is caused by a hormone imbalance which may indicate the presence of a polyp." He put out eight sturdy fingers on two hands, miming the features of an octopus.

"She had been examined in England, several times before."

"I grant it. But she has not been examined thoroughly in the last couple of years. Two months ago I examined her and detected the polyp. Four weeks ago I removed it and put her under the C-5 hormone treatment. It involved the hormone transplant of a female chimpanzee."

"Will it go on long? I mean the treatment?"

"No, the treatment will end with the coming of the New Year. Then she ought to take a holiday, somewhere. We will then see whether the pain and the frequent menstruation will reoccur or not."

Next day Helena visited her friend on her own. She gave me the news as we lay in the wonderful double bed of Azirjan's apartment.

"Tanya is in love." She held my hand, pressed my fingers.

"I take it, it is the Turkish doctor."

"Yes, it is him. But he is a Muslim. Fancy that."

"Would the nondenominational pastor or the church's rite forbid such an association?"

"Not if it leads to conversion."

"How did they meet?"

"For a good many months of the year, Tanya was attending the services of the Nazarene Church." Helena's grip loosened on my hand.

"Who are they, the Nazarenes?"

"A rather curious but impressive Christian sect. They abhor any kind of contraception, so their families tend to have double figures in children. They will not touch weapons; they would rather go to prison in wartime. They would not raise as much as an axe or shoot an arrow." My wife took both my hands in a new, even firmer grip. Was that a sign of approval or disapproval?

"And what has Tanya to do with them?" I enquired.

"According to her, they are the purest of the pure. They don't only talk Christianity but live by it." She let my hand go.

"And the Turkish doctor?"

"He was called to their assembly one day when a woman had collapsed in a fit. He attended to her, took her to hospital— Tanya helped him—and found a cure for her illness. Then Tanya confided in Pamuk, and eventually she underwent the procedures (which you know about) as devised by him."

"What will be the next step?"

Helena did not answer but turned her body around in bed. I think she was guessing an answer but did not wish to come out with it. We went to sleep.

The Longhi picture was valued by Sotheby's in London. If auctioned, the starting price would be two million pounds. Not bad. We could buy a large house with a sizeable garden. We could go on a transatlantic cruise. Or buy a boat. We could put a large nest egg in the bank as Eve's dowry. We could . . .

"We will do nothing," said Helena, resolutely. "We will insure it and hang it up in the living room."

"You are my girl," I said and kissed her. The gondola was now on the wall, the gondolier looking at us while pulling his oars, the Doge's Palace is in the background just under our cuckoo clock.

11. Castelfranco Veneto

"Fair Italy, thou art the garden of the world, the home of all art
yields and nature can decree."
(Byron: *Childe Harold*)

Sissignori, l'Italia è un bel paese,
Ricco di latte e mile, di frutta e fiori,
Pien di saggi, d'artisti, di scrittori,
E grande un giorno per guarasche imprese.

Yessir, Italy is a lovely country,
Rich in milk and apples, fruit and flowers,
Full of wise men, artists, writers,
A grand day for a guaranteed enterprise.
(G.G. Belli)

Like an innocent young girl's breast, the little town of Castelfranco Veneto makes a slightly rising hill on the flat landscape. With a little imagination, the tower of the parish church (calling itself the Duomo) would appear as the nipple on the breast. Approaching it from the west by car, the slightly curving road takes a right to the middle of the town, passing the clinic, a bar, the school, a row of shops, two restaurants and a roadside chapel.

It was a Sunday when we reached Castelfranco, travelling in my Passat, with windows open as the car lacked air conditioning

146

and it was warm outside. I drove really slowly as if unable to make up my mind whether to look for my relatives first or Giorgione's paintings. Everything was unusually quiet. The church wasn't filled (it must have been well after mass), the restaurants and the bar looked deserted, the streets too, except for two old men sauntering on the road, following the curving smoke rising from their pipes. I asked them for directions, which they gave readily, gesticulating with their pipes in hand.

Then I heard a massive sound, like the choir bursting forth in the middle of an opera. I think the chorus said: "GOAL" in unison. They were all in the communal building watching the duel between AC Milan and Internazionale Milano. AC Milan must have scored in that instance. The communal hall had a wide cinema screen for the benefit of the supporters, who seemed to have been rooting for either team in pretty equal numbers.

I imagined Zorzo painting alfresco on the eastern wall of the Fondaco or on the Casa Marta-Pellizzari. He, like any other fresco painter, would have had to work fast on the wet wall so that the paint would stay moist. He would have had to mark the points with almost invisible carbon dust on the mortar. These would altogether disappear under the paint. For oil painting Giorgione used badger hair brushes; for the fresco he used brushes made from the dorsal hair of wild boar.

Giorgione's fresco on the east wall of the Casa Marta-Pellizzari in Castelfranco Veneto is nearly 16 metres long and about a quarter of a metre high. It consists of a series of musical instruments, cameos, books, heads and measuring instruments relating to an astronomer/astrologer—the two were the same in his time. The divination associated with this turn of century representation, and possibly connected with Zorzo's famous painting of *The Three Philosophers*, is essentially pessimistic. And here is a syllogism. Although Giorgione's paintings are full of life, the figures deriving joy from whatever they were doing—concerts, playing solo instruments or singing—the faces *en premier plan* are reflective; the painting as a whole has a darkish tone, and this contemplative near-sadness is also on the faces of the four figures of the Castelfranco Altarpiece.

How did I get there to see it? It was the summer of changing the coins into euros, and the little town's only bank (the only one we could discover, in the vicinity of the railway station) was brimming with people. I'd just managed to obtain enough new money to host a grand dinner in the Ristorante Castelfranco for my immediate family and for the Castelfranco extension. (As it turned out, the lira kept functioning for a good while.) There we were, alfresco, under a huge tarpaulin: Mum and Dad, Helena and Eve, my aunt Giuliana from Venice (her husband Benedetto had died), Giuseppe della Croce (now from Rome), his son Frederico and Giuliana's two daughters, Tina and Nina. The family feud had ended.

Mum and Dad had arrived by plane and were returning to London by air. I was driving my Volkswagen Passat, which had enough room to transport five people for a week and then to take the three of us around for a month.

Although the restaurant was normally a solid middle-class affair, the owner was an amateur lutist and provided us with exquisite background music: Monteverdi madrigals, Orlandus Lassus organ music and Palestrina's Easter mass—all on a long, repeating tape. We had *porchetta*, with *patatine arrosto*, *carciofi*—*minestrone* beforehand and *dolce penultimate* and coffee to finish with. The *dolce* was a large square chocolate cake with "40 *anni*" written in icing sugar suggesting that my parents' alienation had lasted that long. In fact, it was a bit longer, and had ended amicably.

Towards the end of this banquet, the young ones left the table and played basketball behind the restaurant. Eve's radio was blaring pop music, fortunately far enough from us oldies, as we were enjoying our classical music. Immediately after the coffee and not waiting for the liqueur, I stole away from the company and proceeded to see Giorgione's masterpiece in the Duomo di Santa Maria Assunta e San Liberale. It towered over the tomb of Matteo Costanzo of Castelfranco, the son of a general who had been serving under Queen Caterina Cornaro in Cyprus. Of the standing figures on the left, one is a soldier in shining armour (possibly required by the older Costanzo himself), on the right is a monk in Franciscan garb, perhaps St Francis himself. Compared with other representations of the Virgin elsewhere (Venice, Berlin, Bologna, London, Messina), the Virgin is on an extremely high pedestal, which is not altogether explained by the probability that Giorgione placed her on top of a funerary altar, which consisted of two pieces: the lower part a sarcophagus, the upper the pedestal.

While I was discussing the merits of Giorgione's *Pala* with a local art historian, Helena entered the church and joined me. She said, quite boldly, "This is the Giorgione painting I least like."

"Why?" Mario Scalese, the local art historian, was taken aback. Then he added with hurt pride nestling in his voice, "This is the largest of the master's paintings, and apart from those astrological signs, is the only one he graced his own town with."

Helena's reply started on a high note, her soprano voice trembling with unexpected emotions: "No one does the best painting in his own town. Michelangelo was Tuscan, but his Sistina frescoes are in Rome. Although Titian was from Vecelli, all his masterpieces were painted elsewhere. Raffaello was from Urbino, and he ended up as a Roman artist . . ."

"*Signora cara*"—Don Mario's forehead broke out in sweat— "the opposite examples are just as numerous. Take Botticelli, Giulio Romano, Giotto . . ."

I intervened. Disputes over art can be as sanguine as quarrels over rival football teams. "What do you find objectionable in this altarpiece, my love?" (I took her left hand, leaving her right free for gesticulation.)

She used her right index finger for pointing: "Everyone is so very sad. They are almost crying."

"The painting is commemorating a death that occurred in 1504."

"The *Bambino* is not beautiful. Not like in *The Tempest*. In fact, this has the face of an over-precocious, spoilt child. Compare this with the suckling babe of *The Tempest*, who is a natural little fellow."

"That picture celebrates life; this doesn't."

"This *Pala* is extremely formal, and there seems to be little or no link up between the figures in the painting."

"The link up is the young man's death. Symbolically, if not actually, they all think of the early demise of young Matteo Costanzo, in the flower of his youth," I explained.

Don Mario summoned up some courage and opened his mouth. "Indeed, the soldier is Matteo Costanzo. But according to representational tradition, he had to be a saint as well. So the *cognoscenti* say he is St Nicasius. You know the picture hanging in the original Costanzo chapel in the original old church of St Liberalis in Castelfranco."

"These kind of pictures are usually called *sacra conversazione*."

"I don't think the Giorgione *Pala* could easily be called that. No doubt the Virgin Mary and Jesus sit on the top in majesty, and the two saints stand guard, as it were, but there is no visible contact between the top group and the standing figures. Spiritual contact, yes. They all mourn the deceased Matteo. We are looking at a funerary painting in a funerary chapel."

"The figure of the soldier dominates the picture with his brilliantly shining armour. Why?"

"I guess it is deliberate: the soldier represents Matteo. It is his heroic death Giorgione celebrates."

We met my parents at the foot of Giorgione's large statue near by. It showed a barrel-chested, youngish man under a cape, gazing at the poplar trees or even beyond and standing on a pedestal even higher than that of the Virgin in the church. A nineteenth-century effort.

Zia Giuliana and Zio Giuseppe were anxious to show us the ancestral home of the della Croces; Mum, on the other hand, took us to the Palazzo del Monte di Pietà, which used to belong to the Colonna; they are all pictured, in a group, on a large canvas by an unknown painter of good ability. Mamma related that as a child visiting the Colonna palace (later it was inherited by their relatives, the Riccati), she identified the figures on the painting as the members of her own family, the della Croce. Nonno was Don Antonio Colonna, Nonna was Donna Patrizia Colonna, her late aunt Letizia was Annamaria Colonna, and so on. All in the mind. In the evening we all went to the theatre, although it was only an amateur group of wandering actors from Venice who performed a *commedia del arte* comedy. The next day Mum and Dad took me to the cemetery. Eve, who had refused to come, went with her younger relatives for a walk, they called it *circomnavigazione*, around the little town, which patchily had retained part of its one-time city walls.

There was a nineteenth-century grave in one corner of the cemetery—far from the Barbatellas, my relatives—which had the following inscription: *Hic iacet Frederius Zorzon, 1710–1790 RQIP.* Evidently Zorzon was not only the Veneto version of George, as a Christian name, but it also existed as a surname as well.

The *campo santo* was on a gentle hilltop, and the rows of graves were alternating with rows of Cyprus trees. Over the arching gate there was a large inscription: *RESURRECTION*, and there were freshly cut flowers in vases on many graves. One such was the humble grave (with a small marble cross), the resting place of the Barbatella. Dad, who was never forgetful in matters of flowers or plants, planted some geraniums in the soil of the grave. There was also a smallish funerary chapel there showing the fresco of the resurrected Christ, a modern effort by a local painter called Tullio Scalese, the father of the art historian we had met in the Duomo.

Giorgione must have spent most of his active life in Venice itself, partly in the company of his assistant, Titian, and partly on his own—the lion's share of his commissions coming from the citizens of the Serenissima or their associates.

He may have worked for a time in the workshop of his "colleague" Vincenzo Catena; he may even have had board and lodging there, in Catena's house. Castelfranco Veneto—one of the four namesakes in Italy—was a good day's walk from Venice or half a day on horseback. What did he take with him when he temporarily returned home to tackle the fresco job for the Casa Marta-Pellizzari? I guess he had a loose leather bag strung around his shoulder, containing his implements: brushes of all sizes, pulverised paint in tin boxes or in tin tubes, one or two canvases rolled up—to paint the occasional portraits in the breaks from fresco painting—then chalk, carbon and lead and his lute, I'd say. Maybe the scores of two songs he had composed now lost or transfused into other songs and ending up as madrigals under a different name. He must have carried a piece of cheese, a sweet Venetian breadroll and a flask of wine for the journey.

When, the following day we were to pack in order to leave Castelfranco for the Lido of Venice, Helena was nowhere to be found. The town is not big, the shops are not numerous, and we had already seen the sights—where could she be? I sent Eve to search for her mother. She returned within two hours, having scoured the town ("Even an open cistern," she said), but she could not find her.

Then I had a brainwave and went to the cemetery. She was sitting on a grave, with a grave face like the Virgin's from another painting, standing at the foot of the cross.

She was kneeling in front of a very small, freshly dug mound, which had an unusual cross on top of it.

"Was that the wounded bird you buried which you found the day before yesterday?"

She shook her head. Her Madonna face could be that of the Virgin's in the painting.

"No, the wagtail had healed up. I buried my paintbrushes here, except two." She pointed to the thin cross which was constructed of two paintbrushes. "We should all die," she said, "like the paintbrushes."

"But before that I'd like to be at least a grandfather," I answered, and offered her my arm. "Resurrection," I added, and took the two brushes.

153

At the Lido, at sunset, I spotted a guy with fins, goggles and dagger in hand: scuba diving at the end of the pier. When he surfaced he had a couple of oysters in his hand. His wife, or girl-friend, standing on the pier with a net in hand, bagged them. We camped at a nearby hotel. Next morning, just after dawn, I woke Eve, and we went down to the pier. I got eighteen oysters. The *padrona* cooked them in the hotel—as oyster soup. We ate them amidst family cheers.

Next day, working at it steadily, I fished up thirty-five oysters. The *padrona* cooked them in the hotel—as oyster soup. We ate them without family cheers. Eve said: "Oysters? Not again!"

12. Lupus (Taperecorder) in Fabula

"We are the summary of all existence. Love and
hate are nesting in us. Passing judgement,
we attract or repel one another. At the
depth of our soul—like a frog in a well—
a little balance-indicator: conscience dwells."
(Samat Obedbak)

I am not exactly proud of what I did during the following Easter. Tatyana had recovered and returned to London for a couple of weeks, partly to see her father and partly to readjust her PhD project along the lines I had suggested. The new title became: "The Roman Pictures of Giorgione da Castelfranco".

What had inspired me, originally, to suggest this topic was a large print of the *Suonatore di Flauto* which one of my students had obtained from a *bottega* near the Galleria Spada in Rome.

The back of the print had an anonymous Italian poem, written in longhand, whose eight lines I translated into English and placed under the picture which now hangs in our living room. It goes like this:

In your paintings gold and crimson dreams,
Of blonde head of hairs,
Brilliant middays, and happy afternoons,
Sunshine in the island, and also in the heart.

155

> All the sumptuous pride of Venice
> Lives there in colours and in joy
> The blue of the eyes, and of the skies
> Talking of the reawakening of Hellas.

The picture (frame and all plus the poem) covers a cavity we inherited from the previous owners. At the point of purchase I did not insist on the sellers making that good, as I thought it a convenient nook to hide the jewellery Helena had inherited from her mother and grandmother. The hole was large, the jewel box was small. The seller of the house, an old gentleman of eighty-five, explained that it was a shotgun wound in the wall. He once had been keen on shooting pheasants and hares, and once, inadvertently, he brought his loaded shotgun home and hit his living room wall by accident. He too had a picture hung over the cavity.

Tatyana came for lunch to our place one day after Easter. I had met her previously at the university but wanted to see her again. So I stayed home for lunch—*spaghetti alla carbonara* and fruit salad—which Helena had prepared, before I had to rush to the university. The midday traffic to Gower Street was tolerable. The women at home were still in the dining room, Eve was at school, the living room was temporarily empty, but the Gaggia, the Italian espresso machine, was already on the glass top coffee table, and *amaretti* biscuits were waiting for munching in a plastic box. I took the *Suonatore di Flauto* off the wall, placed my prepared tape recorder in the cavity, on top of the jewel box, and sat down for a minute or two. The ladies came back soon. Tatyana's liquorice black hair was put in a pony tail ("*a Turkish flag*", said I). Helena's silky brown hair (recently highlighted, so it shined like the hair of Caterina Cornaro) flew loosely around her Madonna face. I felt a bounder in doing what I did: to record their conversation in my absence. At the time, I justified my operation thus: Helena is mightily upset at the showing up of the Turk—despite the Muslim doctor's positive actions—fearing that her best friend would fall into the large, multifarious Muslim net. Would Tanya be a haemoglobin in the Islamist phlebotomy? In Helena's eyes, Islam was the No. 1 enemy of Christianity.

I returned home after six. In the meanwhile Tanya had departed, Helena had brought Eve back from school, Dad and Mum had called, and the day was as good as done.

Next morning I took the recorder and the tape with me to the university and listened to the conversation of the two women in the privacy of my office. (Should I get my book published, I may apply for a personal chair.)

Helena: "Tanya, how serious is this business with your Turk?"

Tanya (animated): "I wish you'd refer to him by his proper name: Dr Ibrahim Pamuk. Anyway, the business is visceral."

Helena: "OK, OK. Keep your hair on. So, Dr Ibrahim. Are you sold on him?"

(One of them, perhaps Tanya, tapped the table with a silver spoon).

Tanya: "I wish you'd use kinder expressions, or truer ones, for that matter."

Helena: "You did not answer my question, however."

Tanya: "I'll answer it presently. As far as I am concerned, the *business* is serious. The transaction may be for life."

Helena: "You're joking me."

Tanya: "I'm not."

Helena: "In other words, you would like to marry him, would you?"

Tanya: "If he would have me . . ."

(Squealing of car brakes, outside on the street, harsh insistent hooting. I must not forget to put in double glazing.)

Helena: "So it is not yet a foregone conclusion?"

Tanya: "Not that, not yet. When I have sufficiently recovered after the treatment—my period, please God, coming and going regularly with the lunar months—I'll take up Ibrahim's suggestion for a longer holiday in Istanbul."

Helena: "He is from there, I take it. And you've visited there already."

(The chugging noise of the Gaggia fogged up the next two minutes of the conversation.)

Tanya: "His dad is a tailor. He wears a shako-like flat-topped Turkish hat; his mother walks around in red slippers. They are simple, unsophisticated folk. They live in a nest-like little house at the back of a cinema owned by an uncle with a vast moustache."

Helena: "For that matter your Ibrahim also wears a moustache, not the size of a sergeant major's but rather like that of Clark Gable."

Tanya: "He is not as handsome, thank God. Then all the women would be after him."

Helena: "Are you jealous already?"

Tanya: "Yes, I am. *Jealousy is a degree to love.* Or part of it."

Helena: "Would he be jealous of you? After all, as a Muslim he could marry you and take a second wife too."

Tanya: "Helena, you are grossly misinformed. Turkish law does not allow multiple marriages. Saudi Arabian does."

Helena: "But he doesn't live in Turkey, does he?"

Tanya: "He only goes there to visit his family. Otherwise he lives in Milan where the law equally forbids men taking more than one wife. I have not mentioned his sisters yet. Leila, the older—not much chubbier than you—is married to a carpet merchant who has his place in that magnificent bazaar. I bought a small Persian rug there, with red birds flying on it over a green field covered with blue flowers. Leila made several cups of strong black tea for us while we were there. 'Allow me,' I said, fetching a lemon from a fruit store. 'I like my tea with lemon.' I squeezed in some juice, added lots of sugar, and then happily drank her tea. They laughed. They are kind, liberal people. On parting she gave me *halva* and fried dough."

Helena: "That may be, but they are Muslims. Consequently they may not be so liberal in other respects, like letting a Muslim marry, and tolerating marriage to, a Christian girl."

Tanya: "I'll return to that. But first let me tell you about the second, the younger sister. She is called Soraya. She is beautiful, thirty years old and unmarried. She is a lawyer working for a law firm: Muhammad, Murad and Bayazid. Nominally she is a Muslim but without any of the trappings. No purdah, no veil, no shawl or kerchief of any kind, but high heeled shoes and strawberry lipstick. She is funny, quick witted, full of wise cracks and jokes."

Helena: "Tell me one!"

Tanya: "Don't worry about the water. Every water finds its ditch. It is not worth lying. A liar can be caught sooner than a lame dog. The black pepper is small—but forceful."

Helena laughs. Her laughter is a rare bird nowadays. (They are rattling the china. Evidently a fresh cup of coffee is poured, because Tanya is asking for milk. The cuckoo clock above the Longhi picture strikes three times.)

Helena: "I have nothing against his looks. He has a stern, regular face, burning oval eyes, he is elegantly dressed, and he has a handshake like a blacksmith . . . I take it he is settled in Milan. Perhaps for good."

Tanya: "He is settled all right. His rank is registrar, and he is the first assistant, nay, the right hand of the world famous professor Guglielmo Prodi."

Helena: "A brother of the politician, is he?"

Tanya: "I don't know that, but I do know that it was our Prodi who initiated the particular hormone treatment which Ibrahim applied to me. Successfully. Or it appears to be successfully. But the proof of the pudding is in the eating. Could I conceive?—this is the question. Could I go through a trouble-free pregnancy? Time is against me, I am no longer very young. Well, to return to Ibrahim—he has an apartment with two bedrooms in Via Manzoni."

Helena: "Have you ever stayed there? I believe it is a good neighbourhood."

Tanya: "What you want to ask is this: have you *slept with him?* No, I have not. I perhaps would have done. He hasn't asked me."

Helena: "So, it is what they call a platonic love affair between you two. He has not even kissed you, has he?"

Tanya: "He has. On both cheeks. On my forehead too. Not on my mouth. Not yet."

Helena: "Permit me another question. We are after all good friends, even close friends. Even best friends once. Is he not . . ."

Tanya: "He is not. Not gay. He is attracted to me, all right. But he is slow, ponderous. He is not a playboy. He is a doctor, a healer whose principle is 'to ease pain'."

Helena: "Again, do forgive me for these awkward questions. (I hear the furniture shifting under her squirming bottom.) How can you be sure he is not gay? Or asexual for some reason?"

Tanya: "Well, he is a widower. And he touches me, caresses me and kisses me tenderly. And I watch his body language. Recall *The Kermess* by Brueghel? Something happens there with the male dancers' anatomy. Ibrahim's likewise. But he has self-control."

Helena: "So it is a matter of time." (The siren of a passing ambulance obscures Tanya's answer.)

Helena: "As a matter of fact, I am not so much concerned with the physical aspects of things; it is the spiritual aspects that bother me. You have been attending Nazarene services. They seem to be a good crowd, followers of Jesus Christ, according to their own vision. But your *inamorato,* although a good doctor, is a Muslim who denies the divinity of Christ, believes not in the Holy Spirit and worships Allah."

Tanya: "As a matter of fact Dr Ibrahim Pamuk, you say *my inamorato*, is no longer a Muslim, he is an atheist. He believes that Allah, Jehovah or Hari Krishna are human inventions. 'Men are weak, so they need a prop.' This is one of his favourite sayings on religion. He knows that I am a Christian, he knows I revere Jesus who is—to his own Muslim father and mother—just a prophet. I once walked with him past the mosque, near Hagia Sophia, which is now a museum. Ibrahim's dad, the tailor, incidentally Ibrahim Senior he is, was there near the entrance, kneeling on his square mat, headward to the *mihrab*, to the East, praying ardently. His bottom was stuck out towards us outside onlookers. He was just one in a row, in a row of rows; the bottoms looked just like rows of onions in a vegetable bed. I am in no danger of joining them."

Helena: "Nonetheless, I hear that Muslim women regularly have a terrible time, and also women married to ex-Muslims, likewise. Remember Caroline in your class? She married a fellow from Troy, who begat two kids, then—taking the boy with him—went to and disappeared in Baghdad. And another thing. To me the Turks seem to be culturally a cruel lot. Look what they did with Jirar's people, the Armenians, during the first World War. They killed a million and a half of them. The first holocaust it was."

Tanya: "No such thing as *cruel people*. What about the Germans during the Second World War? They gassed and shot seven million people in toto, Jews and non Jews."

Helena: "Not all Germans were killers. Only a crazed bunch."

Tanya: "Not all Turks were killers. Only a misled lot."

Helena: "It is not easy to swallow the *machismo* of easterners. Any one of them."

Tanya (Laughs): "Then you will see one day that this particular *swallow*, which is me, will bring the spring as well as the summer. At any rate, it may not be too hard to follow a man one loves. How about your own case?"

Helena: (The answer is in a voice higher pitched than her normal soprano.) "Do you mean Giorgio?"

Tanya: "Who else?"

Helena: "He is a kind man. A bit pedestrian and predictable. Sufficient in physical strength but not sufficient in artistic imagination."

Tanya: "More brawn than brain?"

Helena: "I did not suggest that. Just that he lacks the flight of creative fancy. I make up for it though."

(At this stage I think a tray comes into operation, with the china and the silver spoons clinking on it. The spoons were a gift from Jirar two Christmases ago. I fear that the women have disappeared into the kitchen to wash up the cups and saucers, but apparently only Helena attends to that task. Tatyana rummages through the old 78 records, finds an early Italian collection of lute playing, and selects a pre-Monteverdi madrigal; and the gramophone faithfully reproduces the sounds Giorgione might have heard and played on his lute. Then Helena comes back, puts on another 78, the *Bartered Bride*, *sotto voce*, and begins her "interrogation" of Tatyana once again.)

Helena: "Tatyana, you have been a missionary. To some extent I may thank my change of heart, and faith, to you. Will you now relapse?"

Tanya: "I don't intend to. Remember my occasional criticism of the practitioners of Born Again Christianity—that they were concentrating merely on Roman Catholics for their conversion? As if they had a mandate to pinch old kinds of Christians, and make them new kinds of Christians. After all, if you worship Christ—from whichever angle—you cannot really be on a losing ticket. I have not heard of a missionary, not in the last few years, who would have gone to a Muslim country to preach the true faith in order to convert Muslims into Christians. As a Jewish Christian, I know this better than anyone."

Helena: "Well, it would be an arduous task to convert Muslims to Christianity. In centuries of hard language, the Christians were called 'faithless dogs' by the Muslims."

Tanya: "There are Muslims, and Muslims. Some are rapacious and aggressive, others are mild and law abiding."

Helena: "Sharia law . . ."

Tanya: "Whichever law. You have a chance with people who are quiet and peaceful."

Helena: "Surely, the Koran sets two standards: one for Muslim versus Muslim, the other Muslim versus Christian intercourse."

Tanya: "This is the hub of the matter. On the one hand, the Koran is open to different interpretations; on the other hand, one may continue to explain to those who are peaceful that there is another holy book that treats everyone equally."

Helena: "I'd like to believe that, but it seems to me that the Bible treats the Jews as people of exceptional merit. The chosen people. Possessors of the Covenant."

Tanya: "Yes, chosen to be the race for the humanity of Jesus Christ. But chosen also for more suffering than any other nation."

Helena: "So, the Old Testament treats people unequally?"

Tanya: "But the New Testament reverses the trend. Jesus and his followers treat everyone equally. Even men and women."

Helena: "May I ask then: how would all of this apply to an atheist, like Dr Pamuk? All is wiped off his slate."

Tanya: "I intend to dedicate the rest of my life to convincing him that humane behaviour, caring and healing, good will and good faith come from God. Yet another thing: I would like to have a child, above all. Could I conceive? This is the question. Could I go through an uninterrupted pregnancy? I must try. Time is against me, I am no longer very young."

Helena: "Should you have a child—could he, would he let him/her keep your faith?"

Tanya: "More than that, didn't I tell you in so many words that I want to convert Ibrahim too? They say that the philosopher Ayer converted from materialism to spirituality just before he died. And as far as certain Muslims are concerned, do you remember that baker in South Kensington? That one near La Bocca? He came as a young Muslim emigrant from Beirut, some ten years ago, then he married an English girl in the Oratory.

Now they have three children. The whole family are Christians."

Helena: "Yes. Roman Catholics to boot. I grant you, they are nearer to the truth than the Allahites. And, I admit, there are decent clerics among them. One of them, called King, pulled out Eve from the Thames. A widower, the successor of Don Ignazio in the Oratory."

(The tape had run its course *suum cuique in viam pacis*). When, a few days later, I met Tatyana again, I could and did refer to her *conversazione* with Helena as if the latter had told me the gist if it. (I was even more ashamed of my stealthy action.) After discussing the religious themes in Giorgione's paintings, I put a sudden question to Tatyana: "Should God reappear on earth today, what would his profession or trade be?"

I was expecting the answer: *preacher*. But she said: "He would be a doctor, a medic, not necessarily a PhD."

The conversation might have continued, but a large thunderbolt interrupted it, and what followed was the howling of the wind, the patter of raindrops on the windowpane, then an increasing deluge of water hitting the window, the walls, the apple tree in the small garden and the wuthering sound of all.

A branch of the old apple tree broke and crashed to the ground. I sawed up the branch and attempted to place the wood into the shed to dry. I could hardly squeeze in: the place was swamped with Helena's old magazines, unused cookery books and a hundred or more bottles of all shapes and sizes—in a heap. The inside of our abode—the realisation suddenly shocked me—wasn't any better. The kitchen surfaces were covered with boxes brimming with corks, leaving only some little elbow space for culinary use. Nonetheless, even in these self-constrained circumstances, she cooked well. The corner table, once for her paints and paintbrushes, was now covered, breast high, with tea cloths—I counted forty in number—towels and spare bed linen. ("My airing cupboard is ridiculously small" was her excuse.)

In a thoughtless rage—having suddenly felt suffocated—I ditched all the corks while she was out shopping.

On arrival, and seeing the cleaned corner, she broke down and cried inconsolably.

"The Cathedral," she sobbed.

"What cathedral?"

"You have got rid of the building blocks of Milan Cathedral."

I did not know. She said she was going to build a cork-model of Milan Cathedral.

To amend for the injury I had caused, I went to Ruby Wine bottling factory and bought a huge box containing 10,000 wine bottle corks. These corks are now lurking under the stairway, waiting to be cathedralised.

13. Rome

"Go to Rome—at once the Paradise, the grave, the city and the wilderness."

(Shelley)

At the time of Castiglione, Inghirami, Sadoleto and Bembo, Raffaello was painting the Vatican Stanze, Michelangelo was covering the ceiling of the Sistine Chapel with cameos of biblical stories, and the Pope, Julius II, like the gargantuan conductor of a Renaissance orchestra, was ensuring that the quality of the artistic output would outlast his reign, and even his millennium. For the sake of the new San Pietro and the ceiling of the Sistina, he abandoned his monumental sepulchral monument. His daughter, Felice della Rovere, conceived in his earlier unholy days, was married to a blockhead Orsini; she consoled herself with concerts and parties, some artistic, some political. In her castle of Bracciano, the door handle opened the double wings of the *sala* to such visiting dignitaries as Ferdinand of Naples (a portly king, ever smiling); the Emperor Maximilian (who needed an Italian translator, though his Latin was serviceable); Louis XII, the French king, full of hot air; Angelo del Bufalo, lover, and ambassador to France; Agostino Chigi (his profile could have been cut in ivory), who was the financial genius behind the superstructure of the League of Cambrai, an effort to reduce Venice to the status of a fishing village and to get rid of foreigners from Italy.

We do now know how many of these august gentlemen had also visited the salon or even the bedroom of Lucrezia, named Imperia, in Via Giulia, but we have a description by the poet Pietro Bembo of her eyes: "When the fire of her eyes lights up, it changes their colour: a dark lake—like Bracciano at the onset of the evening—blue depths, when the lake wakes up in the morning, shadows, signifying sadness, and lightning like joy, joie de vivre, the eyes forgetting all woes."

Helena and I, hand in hand, were taking a stroll down the kilometre-long Via Giulia, starting around the Palazzo (Borromini's) Falconieri and ending up where the Corso Vittorio Emmanuele meets the Aosta Bridge, a stone's throw from Piazza della Rovere.

"Which was Raffaello's house?" asked Helena, touching, caressing the travertine outer walls of a palazzo. "Could it have been this one?"

"Perhaps that one—over there—is built on the site of his house. That might have been the one."

"Did he know Giorgione?"

"Unlikely. In those days Venice and Urbino were quite a distance from one another, even on horseback. We know little about Zorzo. He might or might not have left Veneto as it was a world in its own right, whose splendour he had helped to create. He might have met Leonardo who did visit Venice, and they might also have had a chance meeting in Milan. He would have learnt the representation of nature from da Vinci, who used it as an emphatic background—then Zorzo developed his own style and used it as a foreground . . ."

On the other hand, the figures in front of a background

representing a slice of nature had already been the way miniaturists painted life-scenes in books of hours or in Psalters. These books had been created before Leonardo, Bernini or Giorgione started to work.

"Look up, what do you see?" Helena asked.

"I see the Gianicolo, the highest point in Rome. Imperia, *cortegiana Romana*, was buried there in the courtyard of a monastery."

"Now if I had, for argument's sake, stood on the balcony of the Falconieri Palace, painting the swallows taking flight from the loggia, over the Tiber, in the direction of the mountain, should I have been representing all I could see? Or would I have been focusing on the birds with the Gianicolo in the background?"

"Your viewpoint depends on your will. This turns your head and shoulders. Your will is governed by your inner aesthetic sense and the rounded impression of the animate and inanimate objects you have, in your given mood. With you, the moods are the governing principles," I told her.

"I have not painted anything for years."

"You told me once your reason: pictures race around in your mind and don't settle to be registered. Rome might help you. We shall *now* go up to the Piazza Navona, not far from here. The sight of the four rivers in stone, the fountain and the church of Sant' Agnese: perhaps these impressions might stay with you, entering your consciousness permanently, so that you could paint them."

She had left her pad and watercolours at the hotel, the Albergo Sole in Via Biscione, next to the Campo dei Fiori. On the way to the Navona, we stopped at the Sole to pick up her implements and buy a bouquet of flowers for the majolica vase in our room.

In some ways the Campo was Rome's throbbing heart. Market in the morning with fresh fish, fruit, trinkets, flowers, vegetables—the poor often benefited freely from overripe produce—a completely cleaned piazza in the afternoon, waiting for locals to chat, sit around, and for tourists to gaze at Giordano Bruno's statue and buy fake CDs from chancers.

Eve had been parked for the day with Maria, her grandmother, who stayed at Hotel Minerva at the side of Piazza Minerva, near Bernini's elephant which is carrying an obelisk and has done so for the last three and a half centuries.

At the end of July we were expecting Tatyana Corwen and Dr Ibrahim Pamuk.

This July, of 1998, was hotter in Rome than I could have hoped, heating me up, the Renaissance scholar, when visiting the centre of the world for the first time. Even the pigeons dipped in the water of the Navona; Helena took her sandals off, and waded in, holding the back of the statue of Danubius for safe balance and looking at his symbolic horse.

"Did you know that the Danube is not far from Prague, where I was born, and that the river washes the feet of Bratislava, Vienna and Budapest, and much much further down he/she ends up in three channels in the Black Sea?"

"You know about it more than I do. But let's go and see the Pasquino."

The ancient statue of persiflage and cruel mockery still stood, after two thousand years, at the northern edge of the *piazza* which was a *quadrigae* course at one time. One *pasquil* from the present time, stuck on the breast of the crumbling statue, was a verse about corruption in the Vatican.

"I hope you will not rope the Pope in."

Helena felt inspired and took a leaf from her notebook and

wrote: "*Helena roamed in Borromini's Rome, then went home, to her own dome.*"

There was no way of sticking this ditty on the statue. We did not have a dome, but the Pantheon had one, St Peter's had another, Santa Maria Maggiore had a third one. In Helena's fantasy, all the three were fitted with gas (the prayers of the Catholic believers), and at a convenient point in time, they flew up in the air like balloons over Rome, right up to the moon. It was called *dome landing*. (There is more cruelty in mocking the faith one has left than devotion to the faith one has accepted.) Helena gazed around, marvelled at yellow-pink-orange palaces, touched statues, caressed them like the feet of the Saviour in the balcony of St Peter's, and Bernini's *Psyche* in the Galleria Borghese, and the feet of Moses in San Pietro in Vincoli; she placed herself in the *stanza fresco* at the School of Athens—she was the distant soothsayer of Dodona; she added herself, as the third (this time female) figure on the *Doppio Ritratto* by Giorgione in the Museo di Palazzo Venezia; she was ready to spread her wings and fly down on to the city of Rome from the Pincio (but I held her fast); she washed her face in the Fontana di Trevi and threw the full contents of her purse in it; she accompanied Eve on horseback in the Borghese Park; she fainted at the sight of the pyramidal skeletons in the Capuchin church of Via Veneto; she swam in the sea at Fregene, then got tipsy from the wine. She did all this, and more, but did not paint (except her nails).

I bought myself goggles, a pair of fins and a speargun, and swam out with Eve (now a safe swimmer) to seek out large stones, sunken tree trunks, and to spy fish behind them. In a small cave I speared an unsuspecting octopus.

We had a companion, a blond boy in his early teens called

Mario Belli. He was Agostino and Emma Belli's grandson. Agostino's son, Mario senior, re-emigrated to and lived in Italy with his family. He had a job in Cinecittà setting up and painting culisse. Mario was a strong boy with a beaming smile and a good eye for spearing fish. He got two sea bream which, added to my octopus, made a lovely meal in Albergo Sole where they cooked them for us free of charge.

Ice-cream, bucketsful, came from the tiny *gelateria* ensconsed in the corner of the Campio and the Via dei Giubbonari. Next door, in the evening, Eve wrestled down a full pizza Capricciosa. Mario, still with us, had a wolfish appetite: he put down two *calzoni*.

Helena found a Protestant church for Sunday worship. I went to mass at midday in St Peter's. Maria helped out by taking Eve to the Luna Park in the afternoon, while Helena and I had our *siesta*.

Next day we had a long walk up to the Gianicolo, where I saluted Garibaldi, who was looking down on the Vatican with disdain, and discovered most of my childhood heroes on the way as marble busts, surrounding Garibaldi. There was Cavour with a bunch of fresh cut flowers at the foot of his pedestal, Mazzini with a laurel wreath around his neck, Manzoni, smiling, perhaps thinking of the happy ending of his novel, *I Promessi Sposi*. And many others: Alfieri, Tasso, a certain Pellegri, whose provenance I knew not, and a certain István Türr, a Hungarian general in the Italian war of the Risorgimento.

Although it was late summer and generally very warm, there were two wet days, with occasional light showers, wet glistening pavements on the Via del Corso on which we walked up and down, finding the girls' sideshow, the Standa department store, where my wife bought a pair of white lace gloves. (There was to be a reception at Noantri in the Palazzo Venezia to which we were invited.) We had iced coffee in Café Greco, under the portrait of Goethe; there Eve came with us to have ice-cream, and then we sat under the shade of newly acquired straw hats, out on the Spanish steps. Eve frolicked in the well of Noah's Ark at the foot of the steps. On the way back, I turned left from the Corso to the Piazza San Silvestro, which is lorded over by the Central Post Office. Right opposite, on the near corner, was the small entrance of David Azirjan's antiquarian shop.

But it was a Monday, a rest day for Jirar's nephew, so his business was closed. I pinned a little note on the architrave of his door, giving my name and the telephone number of the hotel. I had no phone at hand to call the next day or the day after. With the Hachas we went to Tivoli. The bus left from a side street next to Termini Railway Station. Helena had bought herself a camera: she photographed the ducal palace, inside and out, made a snapshot of Diana with the ample-multiple breasts, the pond with Neptune, the gargoyles, the singing organ of fountains—which did not sing—the artificial caves, the marble dolphins, monsters and the few living red-gold fish in the pond. We ate salami sandwiches, drank Italian sweet champagne; Eve drank apple juice. On the way home I spotted a nylon bag in her hand, half hidden behind her handbag. It was full of water. And in the water there was a red-gold fish.

"Please, please, please! Don't take it away! I have no pets, not one pet, now I have one. Please let me keep it."

The soft touch that I am, I bought her a fishbowl, some green plants and fish food.

The day after that they went to Ostia as well as to the Lido di Ostia. The women were equipped with gallons of sun cream, and when there on the Lido—as I was told later—they hired a large sun umbrella. I went back to the Galleria Borghese to take stock of the *Il Cantore Appassionato*. And there, in front of the picture, I spotted the familiar figure of Dr Ibrahim Pamuk, who, as it were, covered with his powerful figure a smaller person, dressed in a gold-coloured dress: Tatyana Corwen. The couple were so absorbed in looking at, nay, scrutinising, the young man's portrait, his nine-gallon red hat, his open mouth and cheerful expression, his strong neck and wide shoulders, the powerful index-finger of his right hand governing the rest of the fingers on his chest, his white surplice . . .

Tanya spoke: "You see, Ibrahim, this guy may not have been alone. The surplice suggests that he was one in a choir. Perhaps they were singing in San Giorgio, Venice."

"Perhaps," replied Ibrahim. "But the Christians do not wear hats in church, do they? You took me to the Maria Maggiore, yesterday, to St Paul's the day before, and there were only some ladies who wore hats or veils."

"You are right, as always," she said. "Perhaps he is rehearsing."

"Perhaps. But what do you say to that: the companion piece might have been a lute player. I know it from you, that your painter hero was a keen lute player. Did he paint other pictures of this size?"

"This size? This might be about four feet by three feet, or less. He had painted all kinds of sizes. From the small *predella* to the large Tedesco *freschi*. I suppose it depended on the commission, or the desire of the patron, or his own fancy," said Tanya.

I stepped forth: "*Buon giorno.*"

They turned, showing little surprise. Tanya kissed me on the cheek, Ibrahim shook my hand.

"You were here without letting us know?" I asked.

Tanya turned crimson. "We have been here over two weeks but did not want to disturb you."

"Or else, you did not want us to intrude on your privacy."

"Something like that," said Ibrahim.

"Your wife, Helena, was not altogether happy with our match. So we picked the Registry Office in the middle of the city and got married there," explained Ibrahim.

"On the Capitolium, at the top palace where men and women are wedded—not in heaven, as the saying would have it," added Tanya.

"Did the geese gaggle, as you came out and stood on the top of the stairs of the Palazzo dei Conservatori?" I asked.

"There weren't any geese there in the Campidoglio," said Ibrahim with a long face.

"Is this some kind of a joke?" asked Tanya anxiously. "You're joking me, aren't you?"

"No joke to the ancient Romans. Gaggling geese were a bad sign: danger to Rome and its inhabitants. But no geese, no danger." Amazingly my joke was appreciated with a smile on Pamuk's face. Tanya burst out in a sharp staccato laughter. The penny had dropped.

"Anyway, your cover is broken. Do you feel like socialising now?"

"Yes, in the daytime, until sunset. We have three more days in Rome, then we go to Milan afterwards and live there."

"I have three weeks leave; at the end of which I must return to the hospital," said Pamuk.

"And what about you, Tatyana, what will you do? Will you try and finish your PhD?"

"I will try. Hence my visit here. We have already been to the Spada and to the Museum of the Palazzo Venezia."

Pamuk, using both hands to smooth out the folds of his light flannel trousers, said sternly: "She could, of course, try and get a job in the History of Art department of St Ambrose University, but I think her interest in art is now shared with her developing interest in medicine, or to be specific, in nursing."

She cast her eyes down as if admiring Michelangelo's pavement on Capitol Square, a fantastic abstract design if ever there was one. "No. I haven't got that ambition. I would like to have children. And if motherhood comes, and lets me have spare time, I would like to do nursing at the hospital."

"May I ask where you are staying in Rome? If that is not a secret, still."

Ibrahim answered: "We are in a hotel in Viale Tiziano. This really is Via Cassia. We hired a car on arrival. When we go into the city, we park it under the Borghese Park."

Tatyana added: "It is a very good hotel, with a swimming pool, and the food is champion with champie. Will you come to see us, tomorrow before noon? You could all have a dip in the pool, and lunch, and *siesta* in the garden. There are other guests with young people there—Eve will not be bored. The Tiziano is not far from the Città del Vaticano, so you can take bus 64 and then walk up there."

We did that, Helena, Eve and I, but after lunch, at *siesta* time, I departed for the antiquarian's shop at San Silvestro. The owner, David Azirjan, was standing in front of his entrance directing a couple of workmen who were, evidently, trying to extend the small entrance hall.

"Now that I have all this antique stuff from my uncle Jirar, I need more space. Fortunately for me, the owner of the next door barber's shop has died, and his widow sold me the premises."

I had met David before, as it were fleetingly, in Milan. There he was in a dark suit and wearing a tie. Here in Rome he wore what looked like a grey toga or gown, which at one point he half-divested and donned just a tunic. My wide-eyed amazement at this strange garb was countered by an intelligent remark: "Giorgio—if I can call you that—take note; the Romans weren't fools. The toga is a comfortable dress, in hot weather anyway; add to that the dust coming from the building works—so there you are."

"Is the shop closed until further notice?" I asked.

"It is. We cannot besmirch our patrons. But inside we are free of dust, so you can come to my office and have a coffee there."

We went through rows of books, the shelves climbing up to the ceiling, through a gothic arch, and got into a room where books not only covered the shelves on the walls but were hanging down from the ceiling on shelves operated by pulleys. The "captain" sitting at his desk could pull all the ropes skilfully as if he were adjusting the rigging of a schooner. Beyond the office there was a kitchenette, a toilet and another door to a store room. (It had been the barber's parlour.)

"Any chance that you may know what kind and quantities of antiques you have inherited, and where they are?"

He produced a long alphabetical list on a scroll. Under lot 17 we found the word *Coppa*. "I have five of them; I wish to show you the most curious one."

"The Cellini imitation cup," I wagered.

He shook his head. The large dark cross around his neck tick-tocked, here to there.

"No, that one was sold by my uncle to an American collector. I believe its present home is Denver, Colorado. It is now in the private museum of the Barker family. They have already given a senator to the US legislature. What I am going to show you"—he took out a coloured goblet, labelled with a red ribbon and placed it on his desk—"is this."

"Go on, pick it up!" David sported a schoolboyish grin; his furtive black eyes glistened in the half-lit study. It had no windows, only an operable roof light, which the French called "*vasistdas*", remembering the German occupiers of 1870.

The goblet was massive although it was evidently made of wood.

"Cherrywood," said David. "A unique piece, at least in my experience."

The outside shell of the cup bore the black figure of a Doge of Venice.

"Morosini," said David, and took the goblet from me. "His presence dates this object for me in the 1490–1510 period. Now look."

The cup had a screw top, which gave way, and an eggcup-like layer, with a tiny stand at the bottom, came loose and away. The shell of this "eggcup" showed the figure of a miniature maiden carrying a basket of eggs. Then it was the turn of the third layer: the picture on the shell represented a lad, flute in one hand, crook in the other, shepherding a flock of ducklings, or were they geese?

"The next layer is telling," said David, and rubbed his smallish hands. He was sleek, somewhat taller than Jirar had been, but still half a head smaller than me.

When the next hollow half-egg was taken out, the shell shone with the face of a great lady. Could it have been Caterina? The visage showed a mature but not yet middle-aged lady, perhaps equidistant in age between the Bellini picture, painted from life, and the Titian picture, which was a combination of copy and imagination. There was a sash across and over the well-padded breasts of the lady, with the letters OLOSEJ.

"*Olosej,* what does that mean?" I asked David.

"Please, read the word backwards."

I spelt it out slowly: "J.E.S.O.L.O. Caterina Carnaro's last home!"

We went out to the Corso and had an ice-cream, sitting out in front of the café and watching the women strolling by.

"Are you married?" I asked David.

He pulled a face, narrowed his eyes and pointed to a flock of young women passing by on the other side, near the column carrying St Peter, high above. "Why marry, when one has such choice?" I nodded, but he continued. "I have a fiancée in Yerevan. Now one can more easily come and go to Armenia, since the Soviet Union has been dissolved. She wants to come here to see Rome for herself. Should she like it, she will stay."

Then I said, getting up (he already had paid the bill), that I wanted to go back to the shop with him, if he could find that document that Doctor Armenius, the first noted Azirjan, left to his family and thereby to posterity.

"I have it. You can look at it."

A small search in the store room (lot 3) produced a four-page document on four leaves. The writing was only on side A of the mould-made paper. It was well preserved, and the words were clearly legible—to those who could read them. This "memoir" or "short account" was written in Armenian.

"Could you translate it?" I asked David excitedly.

He shook his head. "My Armenian is not good enough for a faithful, scholarly translation. But I will make a copy of the

179

document for you, and you can take it to a friend of mine, called Tiridates Eseian. He will produce a translation for you, for a small fee."

Eseian, a paper and picture restorer, had his workshop in Via Babino, near the Piazza del Popolo. (Popolo is poplar tree as well as "the people".)

He was on leave.

The Armenian text was followed by this Italian translation:

"Nel 1510 la peste imperversava fieramente nel Veneto. Morosini mi fece chiamare, perchè una delle sue favourite, la cortigiana Cecilia Lusignan, figlia illegittima del defunto re di Cipro, denunciava primi segni della malattia: febbre, mal di testa e brividi in tutto il corpo, dalla testa fino alle dita del piede. Riconobbi, infatti, i sintomi riscontrati dodici anni prima, quando fui chaimato a Roma a consulto con i medici di Papa Roderigo Borgia. Lì io stesso subii l'intera malattia—e guarii, come la metà degli altri pazienti.

Quando, il primo giorno, la esaminai, Cecilia non era più nel fiore della giovinezza. Non le nascosi la mia diagnosi. Il secondo giorno chiamò un sacerdote cattolico, cipriota Greco, e non ebbe nulla in contrario che io ascoltassi la sua ultima confessione. Quando il prete lasciò il suo palazzetto con un piccolo sacco d'oro in mano, Cecilia mi pregò di alleviare le sue pene. Gonfiori piatti, ovali, arrossati apparrvero sui suoi inguini, sulle ascelle e sul collo. Il mio balsamo l'aiutò a mano, sopportare la sofferenza, ma non la guarì. Allora cominciò a parlare di Giorgione o, come essa lo chiamò, di, 'Zorzo'. Di lui mi era nota la fama.

Dipinse Caterina Cornaro, nostra regina di Cipro, a cavallo, creò una piccolo scena della natività, chiamata 'Nocte', che avevo visto a Palazzo Cornaro. Secondo il giudizio di un consiglio di sovrane egli appartenne ai quattro più grandi pittori dell'Italia.

*'La prego, la supplico, lo
Faccia chiamare, o meglio, lo porti qua'.*

Obiettai che ciò sarebbe stato imprudente, perchè la peste era contagiosa. Malgrado tutto andai a vedere il pittore. 'Zorzo', quando lo incontrai, era già altrettanto malato quanto la sua amante, Cecilia, la principessa bastarda. Tornai in gran fretta al palazzetto. Cecilia, ormai al terzo giorno della sua malattia, erà l'ombra di se stessa. Le diedi della gelatina reale da mangiare e la costrinsi di mandarla giù. Mi disse: 'So di essere brutta adesso. Però soltanto due anni fa ero considerate la donna più avvenente di Venezia. Lo dimostrano due quadri di 'Zorzo', Giuditta' e, Venere'.

Poco dopo mi trovavo in viaggio, alternando carrozza, cavallo e portantina, verso Roma, dove la mia moglie italiana Lisabetta e i miei due figli Jirar e Maria già dal 1498 vivevano.

Era il tempo del 'pàpa terribile', allora già vecchio e debole, che voleva consultare sempre più dottori, me compreso. Nella sua anticamera, vicina alle famose 'Stanze'—questo accadde già nel 1511—m'imbattei nel banchiere milionario Chigi. Egli mi portò in Via Giulia, in un altro minuscolo palazzetto, dove viveva in gran lusso la sua compagna: Imperia (Lucrezia)

Cognato, una bellezza di fama mondiale. 'Febbre che sale e scende', disse il finanziere, sospettando che si trattasse di peste. Esaminando peró la cortigiana, non riscontrai segni di peste, solo scosse e brividi, ambedue sintomi di malaria. A Cipro, qualche anno prima, una volta avevo curato con successo un paziente con dosi massicce di vino di chinina. Credo che se avessi potuto iniziare prima il trattamento di Imperia, sarei riuscito ad evitare che la malattia entrasse nel suo stadio fatale. Cosi però, come stavano le cose, non potevo che allungare la vita di Imperia. Ignoro se aveva fatto un ultima confessione, ma so che è sepolta sul Monte Celio, nei conventi di San Gregorio.

Curioso o tipico? Durante una delle mie ultime visite al suo capezzale la cortigian parlò di due quadri di messer Raffaello che dovevano tramandare la sua bellezza ai posteri. Il primo era 'Saffo al Parnasso' nella terza Stanza, il secondo—di cui essa allora potè vedere solo uno schizzo, portato però poco più tardi a termine—reffigurava l'apparizione di Galatea, cavalcante nàiadi tirate da delfini.

Imperia parlava il Greco come il latino, leggeva Pindaro e citava Adriano:
> *'Animula vagula, blandula*
> *Hospes comesque corporis' "*

"Now to my second question," I said after a while, still perplexed by the Armenian text. "An Italian guest waiting for an Italian answer."

David smiled, spread his hands as if he were going to fly, as if indicating that he was not Italian.

"Your uncle was interested in the hidden painting, called *Nocte,* by Giorgione. Have you any references that might betray traces of his interest?"

In silent answer to my request, David produced a bulky album full of reproductions. It was entitled "NATIVITY". Celluloid sacks protected the pictures, perhaps thirty in number, which were arranged, curiously, in alphabetical order. I paid particular attention to representations by Piero della Francesca, Filippo Lippi, Giotto, Leonardo, Raffaello and Titian. Two Giorgione reproductions were placed between Piero della Francesca's and Giotto's contributions. The first of them was known to me: *The Adoration of the Shepherds,* whose original is in the National Gallery of Art, Washington. Yes, it was a "Nativity" but hardly a "*Nocte*". The latter would demand a night sky (the Washington picture had it in light blue) and a scene that would precede even the visitation of the shepherds. The second painting was spot on. We had an oblong *quadro,* with St Joseph and Mary adoring the child Jesus lying on a white sheet placed on the ground. The trio was looked down upon from the night sky by three small flying angels, illuminated by the rays of the invisible moon. In the far distance were mountains and the towers of a faraway settlement. Nearer to us was the inn, under the shade of a eucalyptus tree, while the roof of the stable was nearly above St Joseph's head. The dark tone of the picture was illuminated only by a part of the sky which had a ray of light, Joseph's golden cape, Jesus' body and Mary's kerchief. Behind the Virgin there was a small flock of sheep. But where was the *original* picture? Jirar did not know, David did not know, I did not know. Could this have been the *Nocte* Isabella was looking for in 1510?

I made a black and white Xerox copy of this reproduction.

David enlarged it. Helena, at my repeated request, coloured it with water paint: the sky was dark grey and ochre, the hills were dark, half circled by dark blue waters, the inn and the stable were dark brown like Joseph's head; his beard was off-white. Mary's hair was dark brown, her praying hands skin colour, the child shone brightly, the sheet under him whitely. The ground was dark green, the tree a lighter orange shade. The angels had dark outlines, and the cloud on which three angels were riding had many colours, due to the moonlight—or was it a mysterious light emitted by the unseen star? The clouds had half the colours of the rainbow. From a photographic reproduction one could not judge the make-up of the colours. Her colouring of the *Nocte* was the last time—it was 1998—that Helena touched paint and paintbrush.

Later on I made colour copies of my copies and sent them to friends far and wide.

The first to react was Angelo Miatello from Castelfranco. He guessed that the original was, or might have been, in Dublin: "In some gallery or other." He also had a reproduction and said that the picture expressed "harmony between form and idea". He thought that the painter—in this case Giorgione, or a follower—might have used planks of wood to canalise light or he might have just imagined a source—invisible on the painting—which emitted the right light from above.

14. Dreams and Realities

"Dreams are wishes, and fantasies,
the results of over-anxiousness or overeating."
(Roberto Bentivoglio)

"Nothing ever becomes real till
it is experienced."
(Keats)

A.

We sold the view of Venice after all, through Sotheby's. It was not by Longhi, but Guardi. I am a *cinquecento* man, not a *seicento* expert. Nonetheless, we got a hatful of sterling. One quarter of it was put aside for Eve's dowry—whenever she gets married. Another quarter, à la Jirar, was given to Hammersmith hospital, where she was born fifteen years ago. With the remaining dosh we bought a flat in Rome, where, during the holidays, I am conducting the research for my second book, *Cinquecento Styles: Venice, Florence, Rome.* We have a rowing boat on the sea, a Jag in the garage, and the mortgage on the London house is paid.

Every Thursday evening in 32, Via Cestari, Rome, Helena's salon is open to her friends, who include a modestly famous pianist, a young stained-glass and mosaic artist of reputed talent, my uncle, the retired sabrist, his wife, the President of the bird watching society from England, and a jolly cook, a really fat lady of popular TV shows who also prepares the food for these occasions.

I am a glutton for stuffed eggs and jellied eel. I gobbled up far too much of these one night. So that night I went to sleep with a heavy heart and a mind full of diverse ideas. I do not know, during the period from midnight to 9 A.M. in the morning, how much actual sleep and real dreams covered me (for I kept waking up and drinking San Pellegrino water to quench my thirst) and how long, and in which sections of the night, I was conscious or half-conscious, and in the talons of night-time daydreaming. At any rate, when I finally woke up in the morning, my nightshirt was drenched with sweat.

I was an eagle. At times I was a Roman sign, leading the legionaries, made of brass, with coal-black iron eyes; at other times I was Napoleon's son, the eaglet, a toy in the hands of crooked diplomats; but ultimately I was the real plumed king of the air, and of the birds, surveying the seven hills from above, dropping droplets on Monte Celio, adoring the Campidoglio, then soaring over the Abbruzzi and flying back to the Mediterranean Sea and landing on top of the mast of the ocean liner *Cristoforo Colombo*, moored in the bay of Genoa.

I heard the captain's voice on the tannoy. "*Aquila*, good friend *Aquila!*"

I answered him in my eagle voice, the only language in which I could utter sounds: *screaming*.

The Captain, his brown face furrowed under a snow-white flat cap, continued: "*Aquila cara*, take flight once more and fly right into the past. Find your spiritual brothers."

I gathered strength, plumed my feathers and caught the pieces of meat thrown up to me in my curved beak; I swallowed them, then took off. There were grey clouds above me, and around me, and below me. I mounted one that was driven by a strong wind and very soon joined by another that was dark and ominous and swallowed my great cloud and me. Presently I was in the eye of the storm. With a clap of almighty thunder, the dark, pregnant cloud twained: one part began to lash rain and hail; the other—my part—sought the warmth of the sun. My feathers dried, I became fluff-light, and with a series of sum-mersaults, I was transported to the far side of the sun. I sailed downwards where, underneath me on the green carpet of a huge meadow, the ore of two armies sparkled menacingly. The bright luminance hurt my eyes. I felt I was lost, or so it seemed, high overhead. I could hear my noisy beating heart.

Then I came to. I drank clear water from a nearby stream, and heard the sound of cannon, the clatter of small arms and the shouts of those bearing them. I spotted two shields: on one there were two eagles, twins they seemed; the other displayed one eagle with two heads. A nearby sign gave a geographical focus to the battle of the two armies: it said Könniggrätz. One bellicose sergeant spotted my flapping wings. "Shoot the bird!" he shouted in a suicidal rage, for targeting the living expres-sion of your chosen symbol is targeting your own soul. Fortunately I was faster than the musket shot intended to bring me down.

I flew further into the past towards Prague and perched on the second pillar of Karl's Bridge spanning the Vltava. The water was still so clear you could see yourself in it, and I saw a white, brilliantly sparkling, snow-white eagle. Could it have been me?

Then I spotted an eagle's nest on top of the highest tower of Hradcany, occupied by another white eagle. She sat on her brood, and getting nearer I recognised my wife. She screamed in eagle tongue, as she had recognised me; I screamed back and never stopped. After three friendly circles and three friendly flaps from above, I was once more on my way.

I flew eastwards and, covering a great distance, felt tired for the first time. I found a cavity in a crag of the highest mountain of the East Carpathians and slept there for a time unknown, unmeasured. I woke with pangs of hunger. I hunted for mice, and had already consumed two when I saw a newborn moufflon, as white as a lamb. I grabbed it from its crying mother, took it to the mountain top and opened its juicy entrails. Appeasing my hunger, I contemplated the lack of *bonum absolutum*. What is good for one, it seems, is bad for another. Victory for the Prussians was good for them, bad for the Austrians. Eating a baby moufflon was good for me, bad for the moufflon mother.

I flew on, and on, and on, and spotting the onion domes of churches, I knew I was in Russia. The country was in mourning. The czar had just died, killed by one of the internal heroes for eagle-flight liberty, the Decembrists. But, lo and behold, the czar's shroud also displayed an eagle on a badge, as majestic and as sorrowful as the funerary procession itself.

I cried. Someone shook me, vehemently. It was Helena, my wife.

"Giorgio, Giorgio, you've been having a series of serious nightmares."

"How, how do you know?" I asked her, grabbing her dry hands with my wet hands.

"You've been screeching like an eagle, just like one."

"How do you know how eagles screech?"

"In my dream—having been woken up by yours, and then falling back to sleep—I was an eagle too. I flew over Castelfranco Veneto."

"Is that likely? Could we have shared a dream?"

"I don't know that, but I do know that apart from screeching, you also pronounced the word '*Aquila*'. So this word must have been the cue to my own dream."

"Well, what did the *Lady Aquila* do in her dream?"

"I flew over the village of Castelfranco Veneto, carrying the leaf of a handwritten calendar in my beak. It was the first day of January 1488. I was flying in a time warp of more than five hundred years ago. There was a cottage at the end of the village with a black stork occupying the only chimney. At my approach she took flight. From the top of the chimney, where I had landed, I could see a handsome countrywoman feeding her pigs. Not far away, a tall strong man was whitewashing the walls of the village hall. A stone's throw from there, in the yard of a Cistercian monastery, a bearded monk was giving a lesson in reading to three kids, all about ten years old. The tallest had a writing slate in his lap and—wanting to have a closer look—I left the chimney and floated right above him. He saw me, wasn't alarmed in the least, but continued drawing and using the white chalk deftly; he included me in the picture."

"And what was in the picture?"

"The cloister, the monk in front, the eagle above."

Eve, now fifteen, was with us this summer in Rome. She was now fully grown and as tall as her mother, spoke tolerable Italian and painted tolerable pictures. She did not want to be a painter but a fashion designer. Dresses interested her, and slick fast cars like the Bugatti or the Mazeratti, but—she said—she could be happy with an Alpha Romeo or Lancia. (*Magari*!) And it was a ten-year-old Alpha Romeo Mario had, given to him in June for his eighteenth birthday as a gift to celebrate the good results of his finals. So he was around with his wide smile, bronze skin,

broad shoulders, large hands and his ever-willingness to enter-
tain Eve. Helena was apprehensive—not so much about the
association of the boy and her girl, but about the dangers of an
old car in fresh hands. My own Jaguar was in being serviced at
the time. Eve could not leave Rome with Mario, her mother
decided, unless Mario was to observe the speed of 70 km per
hour maximum on any road, and Eve was to telephone her
mother every hour and a half of the day. Mother and daughter
had mobile phones—I loathe the instrument.

On Sunday we all went to Fregene in Mario's car. There was
congestion on the *raccordo anullare*, so we were cooking for an
hour or so in the old Alpha Romeo before it could spew us out
on to the beach. Cabin, umbrella, gallons of water and orange
juice, and soaking in the tepid water restored our physical and
mental balance. Helena had bought two large grapefruits and a
paper bag full of pieces of cloves. She pushed the pointed ends
of the aromatic spice into the skin of the larger grapefruit until
it was fully covered and looked like the *tartufo*. I was reading a
fat volume of Jorge Luis Borges's prose. Eve and Mario frolicked, within sight, interminably. Eve, from time to time, stood
on Mario's shoulders and then dived into the warm sea, emit-
ting peels of laughter.

At one point hunger got the better of them and they joined
us. Eve wore her white bikini designed and sewn up by herself.
With drops of seawater sprinkling from her suntanned frame,
she looked like a thinner and more youthful version of Venus.
Mario promptly addressed me with exaggerated politeness.

"Sir."

"I've told you to call me Giorgio."

"Ahm. Giorgio, I would like to ask you a special favour."

"Out with it."

"Well. You know I want to be a sculptor, don't you? Earlier this year I won a junior competition with two fish emerging from the sea sculpted first in clay, then in aluminium, who apparently kiss one another in the air. Have you seen it?"

"I've heard about it, but have not seen it."

Eve piped up: "I did see it, *Babbo*. They are killer whales, but not as big, so technically not fish. The material is silver-like aluminium. They are fantastic. A steel rod holds them together."

Mario cleared his throat. "So, there is another competition, August first is the deadline. They are looking for busts. Men, women or animals. The first prize is 10,000 euro."

I was puzzled and curious. "How do I come into this?"

"Eve has told me that I have to ask your permission to sculpt her bust."

"Please, Dad!"

Helena joined in: "You don't mean to do it in a natural state, do you? Because that is out of the question. My daughter must not bare her breast to a man, even though he might be a promising artist."

"Mum, there is nothing in it except the posing." She turned to Mario: "How long should I have to model for you, Mario?"

"If we obtained your parents' permission, I need you for the primary work for no more than an hour. You stand in the sea, over waist high, looking at me sitting in my rowing boat—soft clay in hand. I'd prepare the rough-out. Then I'll work on my own. The finished, polished, glazed clay statue will be submitted to the jury. The first six will get prizes, and a bronze version of them will be cast . . ."

"Out of the question," said Helena in a high-pitched voice, "for every Tom, Dick and Harry to gaze at my daughter's naked breasts."

"Mamma!" chimed in Eve. "Nobody will know who the model was. Mario will not reveal it!"

"Not reveal it because it will not happen. What is wrong to sculpt you in your bikini top? Your shape will show up just the same, and we avoid indecent exposure."

"May I once more plead with you? Botticelli's painting of Simonetta Vespucci is an eternal treasure of art. Canova's sculpting of Napoleon's sister's bust is the most beautiful piece of marble. She had willingly taken her blouse off even though she was a duchess. Raphael's . . ."

"This is not a question of rank but decency. Go along, Eve, stand in the sea as requested, but as you are now: in your bikini."

I looked around the beach. In the Eighties it was a female fashion to expose breasts; later in the era of John Paul II the uncovered teats were a rarity, mostly restricted to mothers suckling their babes.

The young pair disappeared. A little later I could spot a rowing boat, Mario in it, and a bit further on, a young girl standing over waist high in the sea.

Helena took the trouble to check on them by wading into the water. On return she said to me in a quiet tone, "It's OK. She has her bikini top on."

Eve, the apple of my eye. I looked into the past, saw her newborn, wearing nappies, trained for the potty, playing and quarrelling with her friends, having a toyhorse called "purple colt", learning to swim, falling into the Thames and lifted out of it, bringing home her first secondary school report, with top marks (but not in behaviour), getting her golden earrings, taking ballet lessons then getting bored with it, taking violin lessons at Jana's, then getting bored with that too, singing in the school choir, getting her first high-heeled shoes, listening to classical music, half-heartedly, and being enthusiastic about rock, going to a disco, for the first time, chaperoned by her mother, giving me an excessively large bouquet of flowers on Father's Day.

The bust won third prize, 1,000 euro, was cast in bronze, and on the day of Ferragosto, it was exhibited in the Foro Olimpico, along with the other winners. There she was on a plinth: starkers from the waist upwards.

The letter from Armenius, which I possessed in Armenian, had been for long in my memory's back burner. Then, in August 2005, I had a phone call from David Azirjan who, on the following day, handed me the English translation of the letter. It goes like this:

"In 1510 when the plague swept through Veneto, Morosini sent for me because one of his protégés, the *cortegiana* Cecilia Lusignan, the bastard daughter of the late King of Cyprus, had been showing early signs of the sickness. She had fever, headaches and was shivering from top to toe. Indeed, I recognised the symptoms twelve years earlier when I was summoned to Rome to consult with Pope Roderigo Borgia's doctors. I went through the whole illness myself there, and—like half of the other cases—I recovered.

Cecilia was not in the first bloom of youth when I attended her on the first day. I did not hide my diagnosis from her. On the second day Morosini called a Greek Cypriot priest, a Catholic at that, and she did not mind me hearing her last confession. When the priest left her Palazzetto Cipriano with a small sack of gold, she asked me to ease her discomfort. Smooth, oval, reddened swellings had appeared in her groins, armpits and neck. My balsam was helping, not curing her. Then she began to talk about Giorgione or, as she called him, Zorzo. I knew him by reputation. He had painted Caterina Cornaro, our Queen of Cyprus, on horseback, executed a small nativity scene, called *Nocte,* which I had seen in the Cornaro palace, and was judged by a council of ruling women to be one of the four best painters in Italy.

'Please, please, send for him, or better, go and fetch him.'

I said it was unwise because the plague was contagious. I went to see him, though. Zorzo was already as sick as his lover, Cecilia, the bastard princess. I rushed back to the *palazetto*. Cecilia, now on the third day, was a shadow of her former self. I gave her royal jelly to eat, I forced it into her. She said: 'I know I am ugly now but only two years ago I was judged the best-looking woman in Venice. It is attested by two of Zorzo's paintings, *Judith* and *Venus.*'

Soon I travelled to Rome, with a combination of cart, horseback and sedan, because my Italian wife Lisabetta and my two children, Jirar and Maria, had already lived there—since 1498.

This was the time of the *Papa Terribile,* already old and pretty weak himself, who wanted to consult more and more doctors, including me. In his antechamber, next to the famous *Stanze,* I bumped into the millionaire banker, Agostino Chigi. That was already in 1511. Chigi took me to Via Giulia, another smallish *palazetto*, where his girlfriend, the world famous beauty, Imperia (Lucrezia) Cognato lived in luxurious circumstances. 'Fever, off and on', said the financier suspecting the plague. But when I examined the *cortegiana*, I found no signs of the plague, only shaking and chills, symptoms of malaria. Once before I had treated a patient in Cyprus successfully with large doses of quinine wine. I believe that if I had started my treatment on Imperia earlier I could have prevented the illness reaching its fatal stage. As it was, all I could do was to extend Imperia's life. I do not know whether she made a last confession or not, but I do know that she is buried on Monte Celio in the cloisters of San Gregorio.

Curious or typical? During one of my last visits to her bedside, the *cortegiana* talked of two pictures by *messere* Raffaello, which were to preserve her beauty for posterity. The first one was *Sappho on Parnassus* in the *Stanza,* the second—only a sketch she saw at the time, but finished soon afterwards—was the appearance of Galatea, riding on shells, pulled by dolphins.

Imperia spoke Greek as well as Latin, read Pindar and quoted Hadrian:
'*Animula vagula, blandula*
Hospes comesque corporis . . .'
(Little charmer, wonderer, little sprite,
Body's companion and guest . . .)"

15. Dublin

"If literature is the Irish ideology, what was painting?"
(A question posed by Hugh Maxton)

I kept my ear to the ground. And that's why I went to Dublin to meet Tommy, the writer.

"Have you noticed that the father, the mother and the child formed an almost perfect triangle in the picture?" he said. (He was talking of the *Nocte*.)

"I have seen it but not really noticed it on the reproduction. Is it something significant, you think?"

He put two index fingers together. "Rather. It is the earthly parallel of the heavenly triangle formed by the Father, the Son and the Holy Spirit. And more than that: there are three heavenly angels, three largish clouds and . . ."

"And more than three sheep. The multiplication of sheep may be accidental. Surely the painter was concerned about conveying an intimate nativity scene with an adequate background . . ."

"And succeeded. There is tenderness in Giorgione elsewhere too, but here the tenderness is ameliorated into love, the same love of the infant as portrayed in *The Tempest*, yet even more so. There the shepherd-soldier (or father) is a distant figure, dispassionate; here St Joseph is the best drawn, best coloured, most important figure. This is one of my favourite Giorgione paintings."

Tom, my host, sat back in his armchair and moved the marble queen on his chess-coffee table, although we weren't playing a game. We were speculating on the whereabouts of the original painting whose copy was the *Nocte* reproduction. He was sure he had seen the painting (or another copy of it?) in the company of Father Daniel, the miniature professor of Old Testament studies at St Patrick's College, Maynooth, Co. Kildare. Father Daniel was a collector of paintings, an amateur art historian and a first-class raconteur. He had retired ten years ago and become a parish priest in Kilterran or Kilterreen, Co. Offaly. While still an active professor, and simultaneously, Tom was an active chief librarian, the two went around town and country, seeing galleries and visiting great houses, attending auctions for pleasure at Miley's, and exploring private houses while hunting down, admiring and taking note of Renaissance and Post-Renaissance paintings.

"It was, and still is, a hobby of mine," said Tom, and poured me coffee brewed in a test tube like in a retort. It was Lavazza accompanied by *amaretti*. I looked around in his country apartment. The ceiling of the living room was covered with the reproductions of the Sistine Chapel vault. The walls bore about a hundred reproductions of paintings by such artists as Bellini, Leonardo, Raffaello, Giorgione, Dosso Dossi, Titian, Catena, Carpaccio and some others of roughly the same period, as well as some abstract paintings by his own daughter.

"And the *Nocte*," said I, inspecting the pictures one by one; "where is that?"

"The nearest I got to it is *Il Tramonto* over there." He pointed to a corner where a very good facsimile decorated a segment of the living room.

"I paid ten pounds for it to the London National Gallery."

"How come," said I, "that a person keen on registering Renaissance pictures in Ireland, and claiming to have seen the *Nocte,* can neither recall from memory the picture's whereabouts nor possess a copy of it?"

"Simple," he said, and smiled. While doing so he reminded me of a portrait of Gogol which was a frontispiece in my copy of *Dead Souls,* bound in leather. "I had a heart operation, a bypass, as they call it. They had stopped my heart, replaced four arteries from a long vein taken from my left leg, then restarted the beat of my heart with an electric shock. I regained consciousness only thirty-six hours later, having lost a chunk of my memory. I was away far too long in *netherland.*"

Hmm, I thought. The memory, or the loss of it, plays tricks with one. Tom was an authority on the books of hours—he kept seventeen copies of the *Heures* that he had obtained from six countries—he could, and did help me with the "Gonzaga book", yet he was now at a loss with the *Nocte.*

The apartment consisted of five rooms, the other four laden with books, some of which adorned the toilet too. The books on art—well over a thousand—were of no help; neither was the internet which we consulted up and down, far and wide, in and out, exploring cyber space and the 1,646 references on Giorgione's *Nativity* or the *Nocte.*

It was late autumn of 2006—just a few months ago. The white tree outside had lost most of its leaves, and the starlings noisily inhabited its branches. The lovable, gentle early autumn was turning into a blowsome wet fall. The fanciful clouds knitted themselves into a dull grey blanket on the sky, and the wind caused the occasional house alarms to shriek as if robbers had tried to break into the peaceful dwelling places.

"But what about your list?" I chanced.

"The list of the Renaissance paintings in Ireland is lost—or was stolen. I have had twenty-nine guests in this house during the past twenty years; you are the thirtieth. You, Giorgio, are a scrupulous man, but some of my guests weren't so particular. I never take a book outside this house, yet I lost one with twelve eighteenth-century etchings. A signed poetry book from Seamus Heaney has also disappeared."

"So what can we do?"

"Well, one of two things, perhaps both. We can try and revisit the collections where I have been, and we can look up my one-time companion, Father Daniel, in his parish. He had had a fantastic memory."

Next day, with soft rain dogging our heels and clouding our vision, Tom and I went to the National Gallery. There were three remarkable G.B. Shaw portraits decorating the walls, and the great dramatist stood to attention twice as a statue, proclaiming that it was his money which started this building and made its contents bloom. Yes, there was a Bassano whose colours sparkled darkly, a freshly cleaned Caravaggio, which a bold art historian had identified on the wall of a refectory of a Dublin chapterhouse, and then engineered its transfer to the gallery, a Raffaello drawing ("I couldn't find it in the complete catalogue of Santi's work," said Tom), a splendid, unmistakable Titian, two El Grecos—but no trace of the *Nocte* or even the name of Giorgione. We knocked on the office door of Dr Sergio Benedetti, the caretaker of Renaissance paintings at the gallery. The Florentine gentleman, well dressed in a wood-pigeon-grey suit, was polite but curt with us. He was filled with *hubris* and made us know in no uncertain words that we were on the wrong track: there were no Giorgione paintings in Dublin, and the

199

information which was derived from an exchange of letters with Professor Angelo Miatello in Castelfranco was a mistake or, at least, a supposition.

"When we cannot find something, we tend to name a distant place as its whereabouts," said Dr Benedetti conclusively.

We had a good and expensive lunch at the gallery, then Tom went home to Newcastle, Co. Dublin, to await his girlfriend, while I motored down to Kilmore Quay near Wexford.

When I came to Dublin, at his invitation (by car to Holyhead, ferry to Dublin port), it was made clear to me that my two weekends in Ireland should be spent alone and away from his abode. Tom was a widower, two decades older than me, with a girlfriend younger than me, a Polish girl, the daughter of an army officer, who also cleaned his apartment. I never met her but saw her photograph on the mantelpiece: she had long flaxen hair and forget-me-not blue eyes.

Kilmore Quay for me was one of the dreamland ports, where portly fishing boats cut the green sea into *Möbius-strip ribbons,* and fish galore was the dividend the sea paid for the fishermen's toils. When I got there it was dark. I found a B & B, then a restaurant where I ate monkfish, served by a young lady with trim ankles. After two pints of Guinness, I was ready to go to sleep, yet sleep eluded me for a while. I was thinking of my family—mentally surveying each member, as it were, one by one—and only when I came to the conclusion that they were safe (even in my absence) did I proceed with my night prayer that closed the day. Eve, the apple of my eye, had set her sights on anthropology at Cambridge. She had just achieved the necessary qualifications, a year earlier than most, and when an aging professor interviewed her, she only had to smile. She had the smile of Julia Roberts, but in a younger edition.

Helena, alas rotund and retaining her undulating moods, from the trough to the crest of the wave and back, had devoured several dozen classics and then enrolled to read English at London University. During the day—really any day—I had not been thinking of her, but at night I was missing her quiet breathing and the proximity of her warm body.

Her mother and aunt had bought a house jointly, about a year ago, near to us in the same locality in Fulham. Maria's second husband Dr Hacha had died (a shadowy figure for me, I hardly knew him), and she moved back to London with Jana (who had sold her Milan property), now arthritic and unable to hold the violin, even for teaching. But her right hand was OK, and she was currently busy writing her memoirs while listening to Bach. The sisters frequented concerts whenever they could and paid at least a short visit to us, every other day.

My father and mother were ensconced in a comfortable nursing home in North London. They had two rooms with a bed in each. Mum had a double bed—and when I happened to visit them one day, relatively early in the morning, Dad was in Mum's bed too. They were holding hands.

Tatyana's dad had died, and her husband had become a professor and a leading surgeon in Milan. They had a little boy, called Ibrahim junior, who could speak three languages perfectly: English, his mother tongue; Turkish, his father tongue; Italian, his "national language" because he was born in Italy.

When I was a little boy I prayed thus: "Please God, don't let me die. Should the world end while I am still alive, I could be spirited straight away and translated into heaven." With the years passing my prayer has been modified. Everyone I loved had at least a short supplication dedicated to them, followed by one last sigh: "Let me die first before my daughter or my wife."

Next morning the sun smiled on the small green-grey-black ripples of the sea. She was not baring her white web teeth: Captain Kelly of the *Dolphin* declared deep-sea fishing possible. There were fishing rods and life jackets on deck: the first were needed, the second not. We rushed out, at full speed as far as the Saltee Islands and a little beyond, and then chugged around them. Being October the seawater was near freezing, but I caught two pollock, a sizeable cod and an eel as the day's taking. Compared to the 100 euro I had to pay for hiring the boat, it was small fry, but measured to my expectation that I might not get anything out of season, the catch was tremendous.

Next day it rained ceaselessly, the drops driven by high wind so that even walking on the seashore was unpleasant. I drove to Wexford, had an Irish coffee at the Tower Hotel restaurant, bought a silver bracelet for Eve, a necklace for Helena, and read a book by Beata Bishop entitled: *A Time to Heal*. A dietary triumph over cancer. No one had that killer disease currently amongst my loved ones, but who knows? Extending life by healthy living is *numero uno*.

On Monday, Tom talked about the Beits. The National Gallery had its Beit wing, and the best pictures were housed there. Sir Alfred Beit's granddad had diamond mines in South Africa. He was a pal of the famous or infamous Cecil Rhodes. The grandson bought Russborough, an eighteenth-century mansion on the right bank of Lake Blessington and filled it with masterpieces of paintings. There was a Honthorst, a Vermeer, four Murillos and a hundred more scintillating, world famous pictures, covering the walls of the reception rooms, salons and the dining area. One day the IRA burst in, the old couple were tied up, and their best twelve paintings were taken away. When, after further robberies, the paintings were eventually found, Sir Alfred donated them, and the remainder in the house, to the National Gallery. Since then the chateau has only luxuriously painted bare walls.

"Could it have been that—before the robbery—they had owned a Giorgione, namely the *Nocte*?"

"It could not have been," said Tom, caressing his grey moustache. "That particular house with all its contents is lodged in my memory, unimpaired. There was no *Nativity* there."

"So how do we proceed?"

We went to the Hugh Lane, alias the Municipal Gallery, near the 1916 Memorial Garden of the city. A stretching Rodin youth welcomed us. He was cast in bronze. (How many casts were made by Rodin?) The gallery had a rich levy of impressionist delights and some modern horrors, patches upon patches of paint, each more conceptual than painting. We escaped to the dining area, had a quiche Lorraine and a coffee there, then went back to the impressionists to rub out the memory of the conceptual horrors and fill up with delight.

Perhaps it is a wild goose chase, I thought at night. Yes, if I ever find the *Nocte* my second book would be crowned by a *capolavoro* of a discovery. Even if the painting itself was not necessarily a *capolavoro*. I had the pleasure—or was it that?—I had the curious experience of being on my own. A family man, a teacher, a sociable creature finding the unusual gem of solitude. As if looking at oneself for the first time: from outside, from an unknown angle.

When we look upwards or inwards, we realise that our personality has a centre which governs our attention not only to given details, but also to the area of our whole mentality. When looking out or down, one normally focuses on the task before one—our consciousness is at war, but somewhat in the fashion of pre-programmed robots.

That day we went home and drank a slim bottle of brandy called Miraculum, a product of Hungary from Muscatel grapes. Tom is Hungarian, but a British subject and an Irish librarian. One of his life's works is the unready but continuously researched *Bibliography of St Peter's*, an excuse-project to visit Rome as often as he can.

I don't know how the Celts and the primordial stone-age people moved about in Hibernia (Ogygia to Ulysses), but as far as I, an Anglicised Italian, was concerned, my movements here were controlled by the weather. Next day we went to the Park. Tom had taken time off partly for my sake, but also professionally; he had commissioned himself to see the classic first editions collection in Phoenix Park's Ivy House. The house, as well as the neighbouring Farmleigh House, were once in the possession of the Guinness family of untold riches, both abodes containing pictures of all values and periods. Now in the hands of government departments but still attended by *ciceroni*, the collections were well maintained, the pictures were expertly cleaned, the books were regularly dusted. No Giorgione painting in either of them. A guide suggested that we try the castle of the Earl of Ross, near Boris-in-Ossory. But before that journey we visited Slane Castle, where the pheasants proved to be more numerous in the park than the old books or pictures in the castle.

We spent an agreeable half-day at Malahide Castle, whose one-time owner was a Catholic-Protestant turncoat. In the Battle of the Boyne, in order to retain his property, he had changed sides. We had a look in Ardgillan, for architecture, not for pictures. We climbed the mountain at Bray Head and examined the picture contents (even the stores) of Kilruddery—the lord being both gracious and magnanimous with his favours of politeness. Then we drove to Birr Castle, where the Rosses (and their hounds) resided. Lord Ross was a kind stick insect whose main concerns were two: 1. to restore the world-famous telescope of his grandfather, and 2. to import as many rare plants and trees to embellish his grand park as his purse would allow. Lady Ross, once a country belle, was a different kind of person: someone who was (whose character was) carved of ebony. Apart from presiding over the household and the estate, she was a very active amateur painter who had painted the libraries of twenty-eight castles and great houses of Ireland. She assured me—while serving us coffee with pine-honey instead of sugar—that none of the great houses had a Giorgione picture. "You have to look elsewhere," she said with a wide smile which sat on her face like a jewel.

We were, we happened to be, in County Offaly, and the afternoon had cut itself short; dusk, then early evening set in. Should we call on Father Daniel, unannounced, as it were? We need not have worried. The parish priest was a young man, the chaplain even younger—Daniel had retired, and gone to a nursing home in County Kildare.

Then came the second weekend. I ventured out without a raincoat, visited Hollywood (the original one, not the star-infested rich land in LA), then Glendalough, the first monastic city (now a well-maintained bunch of ruins) in Ireland, where I tried angling in the upper lake, without any success, and got absolutely drenched at the end of the day.

I phoned home at night. Realising that I had never been on my own for any longish stretch of time, I was missing my extended family. Dad said, "Make note, Giorgio, that you bring a bunch of shamrocks home with you. I suppose that will bring luck."

Helena said: "I'm missing you, Giorgio. The course is not difficult, but writing essays is a hard task. Listen to this:

> Beowulf must have been a wolf
> Shakespeare shook his spear
> While writing essays for English lit.
> I shed many a salty tear."

Mum said: "Don't forget the sixth of December, Niccolò. You come along with your Jaguar and take us out. Perhaps to Kew Gardens. Your father would especially appreciate that."

Jana said: "I have composed a little song, Giorgio."

"Play it to me over the telephone."

"I can no longer play. Maestro Rheumatics has stopped me. But I can sing." She sang the little ditty. It was more Sinatra than Janáček.

Eve wasn't available. Her mobile was powered off. She must have been partying somewhere.

Tom had meetings next day, so I had to go and see the old priest with my friend's best wishes and recommendation. The old codger now lived in Clane, a small town on the left bank of the Liffey, and he stayed in a spacious room to himself in the nursing home. He was as little as a dog sitting. The small man was infirm but *compos mentis*. Oh yes, Tom was a cherished memory for him, and so were their art trips together. On the north wall of his room hung two pictures, a grazing cow on one of them, two grazing cows on the other. "Cuyp," said the old priest, and with the rays of the sun seeping into the room (surely the pictures should have been shielded), he caressed his cows with his frequent glances.

"I came from a small farm in County Cork, and as a boy I was milking them."

"They are Dutch classics. They are worth millions."

"When I die my nephew will inherit them."

I showed him the reproduction *Nocte*.

"Oh yes, I know it. Or at least I know a nineteenth-century copy of it. It was in the museum of St Patrick's College, among other relics, antiquities, science history pieces and useless clutter."

"It was? Where is it now?"

Father Daniel lifted his watery eyes upwards. "Who knows? The museum was robbed. They opened up the roof, came in, and took some twenty items, the painting amongst them. Still, plenty remained and are housed safely now. Vestments received from Elizabeth, Queen of Hungary, a letter from Henry VIII of England concerning the founding of Trinity College, Dublin, and other curios."

I shook like a leaf in the wind. "Father Daniel, are you serious? The *Nocte* by Giorgione has disappeared without a trace?"

"That picture has disappeared, but I doubt if it was done by Giorgione's own hands."

He had a head like a lion with a frizzy mane and eyes both wild and tame. "I remember the Maynooth copy of the *Nocte* had a frame. That dusty old golden frame had a label—*Murphy and Mullally*—printed on it. They were a nineteenth-century Dublin firm of picture framers. Excuse me, friend, I have a mass to celebrate in the nursing home's chapel. You can come along if you wish."

I did.

That night, my last one in Newcastle, Co. Dublin, in Ireland, I had a dream which restarted after my awakening at dawn and lasted until the alarm clock interrupted and ended it.

I sat on the shore of the Adriatic Sea, listening to its music to which the tunes of an Aeolian harp were added, making the seacoast Nature's symphony orchestra. There were seagulls in the air, swooping down to take a fish or two from my hands, singing tunes of a Monteverdi opera in human voices: soprano, alto, mezzosoprano, basso. Then a tall man came along, lute in hand. He wore a doublet with a wide lace collar and a soft round hat. A pair of pantyhose on his legs, one red velvet, the other blue. He had a multicoloured feather in his cap, a bag on his left shoulder. He had yellow chamois leather boots on his feet. He did not see me. He settled in the shade of an oak tree, took out a folding card and a set of brushes from his shoulder bag. The sea was swinging and rocking driftwood. The painter fished out a flat piece—perhaps it was a plank of pine wood—and dried it with his breath. But there was no paint about, not even a cuttlefish to provide him with ink.

I squirmed. Slowly approached him. Coughed. Spluttered. Cut my finger on the blade of a sharp seaweed. He had red paint now, from me. The contact has been established between Barbatella and Barbarella.

Glossary

A

amicizia: friendship
A che dice: Who are you telling; don't say this to me
Annamo a casa: Let's go home
aquila: eagle
ardea significant tempestatem: the white heron signifies storm
atra cura: heavy burden, worry

B

babbo: father
bebe Barbatella: Barbatella baby
bene: all right
benissimo: very well
bocca, la: the mouth
bonum absolutum: absolute good
bottega: shop
Buon giorno: Good day

C

cacciatore con polenta: hunter's style meal with polenta
calzoni: folded-over pizza, literally shoes
campagna: countryside
campo santo: cemetery
capolavoro: masterpiece
cara: dear, beloved
carciofi: artichoke
casa dei forestieri: guesthouse
cena: supper (Last Supper)
che bel marmo rovianati: you've ruined a lovely piece of marble
chiachierare: to chat
Che sarà sarà: What will be will be
cinquecentesco: sixteenth century
cognoscenti: people who know

coppa: cup, chalice
condottiere: mercenary captain
cortegiana Romana: courtesan of Rome
clausura: restricted access
culisse: coulisse

D
dolce: cake
dolce far niente: sweet doing nothing
dona nobis pacem: give us peace
Domina Aceli, signora di Asolo: the ruler of Aceli, Dame Asolo.

E
en premier plan: in the foreground

F
faccia, la: the face
feroson: stimulant
Ferragosto: mid-August feast of Our Lady
festa degli ucelli: feast of the birds
festa degli umani: feast of the people
frutta di mare: fruit of the sea

G
giocare: to play

H
Hypnerotomachia Poliphili: Poliphilo's Strife of Love in a Dream

I
inamorato: loved one, lover
I Promessi Sposi: The Betrothed

K
kumis: fermented mare's milk

L
Lege artio: binding
Libro d'Ore: Book of Hours

M

magari: I wish it could be

maggiore/minore: senior/ junior

messer/messere: master

mihrab: a niche in the wall of a mosque, which points to Mecca

molto: very much

N

navigazione fluviale: river cruise

nocte: night nativity scene

nonna, nonno: grandmother, grandfather

O

ohne genier: no bother

ospedale: hospital

P

padrona: landlady

pala: originally meaning blade; here it refers to the altarpiece

palazetto: small palace

patatine arrosto: roast potatoes

pasquil: satirical writing posted in public

piazza: public square

pentimento: literally, regret; visible trace of earlier painting beneath
 the layer or layers of paint on a painting where the painter has
 corrected an earlier version on the canvas

porchetta: a savoury, fatty and moist boneless pork

predella: prayer stool

Q

quadrigae: four-horse team

quadro: painting

R

raccordo anulare: road encircling Rome

ravioli con ostrighe: pasta parcels filled with oysters

ragazzo: boy

S

sacra conversazione: sacred conversation

sala: room or hall

saltimbocca Romana: veal, prosciutto or ham, and sage, rolled-up and cooked in Marsala and butter; literally, jumps in the mouth

Segafredo: a type of coffee

seicento: seventeenth century

sfumato: blending of colours

simpatico: likeable, compatible

sindaco: mayor

soggiorno: stay

spumato: frothy

stanza fresco: room with fresco

stekka con fettucine and carciofi: beefsteak with pasta and cauliflower

Strega: orange-flavoured liqueur, literally witch

studiolo: study

suum cuique in viam pacis: give to each in the way of peace

T

tartufo: an ice-cream dessert

tondo: an oval painting

torta: cake

totum factum: *literally*: a person responsible for everything

tramontana, la: the north wind

tramonto, il: the sunset

tutto in ordine: all is well

U

una carezza: one caress

una nocte, molto bella e singulare: a nativity scene, singularly beautiful

V

vaporetto: water taxi

vasistdas: a whatsit, and a rooflight

veduta: view

veni, vedi sed non vici: I came and saw but did not conquer
vitello tonato: dish of veal and tuna

Z
zabalione/zabaglione: a kind of pudding
zazzera: shock of hair
zia, zio: aunt, uncle
zitto: hush

Paintings

Agglomerato ai Bordi di un Fiume: Gathering at the Bank of the River
Allegoria della Castita: Allegory of Chastity
Il Canale Grande con Gondole: The Grand Canal with Gondolas
Il Cantore Appassionato: The Passionate Singer
Cavaliere di Malta: Knight of Malta
Cerere: the Goddess Ceres
Il Concerto: The Concert
Doppio Ritratto: Double Portrait
Giudizio di Salmone: Justice of Solomon
Guerriero con Scuderio: Knight in Armour
Mosé alla Prova del Fuoco: Moses at the Trial of Fire
*Paedaggio con Giovane Madre e Alabardiere: Landscape with Young
    Mother and Soldier with Halberd*
Pastore con Flauto: Shepherd with Flute
Ragazzo: Boy
Ritorno di Giuditta: Return of Judith
Ritratto di Antiquario: Portrait of an Antiquarian
Ritratto di Giovane Uomo: Portrait of a Young Man
Samsone Deriso: Samson Humiliated
Suonatore di Flauto: The Flute Player
La Tempesta: The Tempest
Il Tramonto: The Sunset
Le Tré Étà delle 'Uomo: The Three Ages of Man
La Vecchia: The Old Lady
Venere Dormiente: Sleeping Venus

SOME OTHER READING
from

BRANDON

Brandon is a leading Irish publisher of new fiction and non-fiction for an international readership. For a catalogue of new and forthcoming books, please write to Brandon/Mount Eagle, Cooleen, Dingle, Co. Kerry, Ireland. For a full listing of all our books in print, please go to

www.brandonbooks.com

NENAD VELIČKOVIĆ
Lodgers

"Nenad Veličković offers a beautifully constructed account of the ridiculous nature of the Balkans conflict, and war in general, which even in moments of pure gallows humour retains a heartwarming affection for the individuals trying to survive in such horrific circumstances." *Metro*

ISBN 9780863223488

AGATA SCHWARTZ AND LUISE VON FLOTOW (eds)
The Third Shore Women's Fiction from East Central Europe

The Third Shore brings to light a whole spectrum of women's literary accomplishment and experience virtually unknown in the West. Gracefully translated, and with an introduction that establishes their political, historical, and literary context, these stories written in the decade after the fall of the Iron Curtain are tales of the familiar reconceived and turned into something altogether new by the distinctive experience they reflect.

ISBN 9780863223624

DRAGO JANČAR
Joyce's Pupil

"Jančar writes powerful, complex stories with unostentatious assurance, and has a gravity which makes the tricks of the more self-consciously modern writers look cheap ... Drago Jančar deserves the wider readership that these translations should gain him." *Times Literary Supplement*

ISBN 9780863223402

WILLIAM WALL
No Paradiso

"In addition to the author's alert, muscular style, his painlessly communicated appreciation of obscure learning, his vaguely didactic pleasure in accurately providing a sense of place, many of these stories are distinguished by a welcome engagement with form . . . In their various negotiations with such tensions, the stories of *No Paradiso* engage, challenge and reward the committed reader."
The Irish Times

ISBN 9780863223556

DAVID FOSTER
The Land Where Stories End

"Australia's most original and important living novelist."
Independent Monthly

"A post-modern fable set in the dark ages of Ireland. . . [A] beautifully written humorous myth that is entirely original. The simplicity of language is perfectly complementary to the wry, occasionally laugh-out-loud humour and the captivating tale." *Irish World*

ISBN 9780863223112

BARRY McCREA
The First Verse

"An intoxicating tale of a young man drawn into a bizarre literary cult...A clever satire of literary criticism, it's also a coming-of-age (and coming-out) tale, a slick portrait of 'Celtic Tiger' Dublin and a compulsive thriller."
Financial Times

"Entertaining, smart, and very, very readable. *The Irish Times*

"An audacious, kaleidoscopic blast." *Sunday Business Post*

ISBN 9780863223808

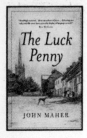

JOHN MAHER
The Luck Penny

"John Maher confirms himself as one of Irish writing's bright stars with this meditation on death… [A] superbly executed story about bereavement told through characters that intrigue from the first... *The Luck Penny* is an outstanding Irish novel for the wider English-reading world." *Sunday Tribune*

"An expertly crafted, tender tale of grief, language and land... A richly rewarding read." *Metro*

ISBN 9780863223617

DOUGLAS A. MARTIN
Branwell

"A tender, tragic portrayal of a doomed artist." *Publishers Weekly*

"Martin avoids the temptation of plunging headfirst into the gothic, instead conveying Branwell's psychic turmoil in simple, stripped-down sentences . . . [He] sparsely fills in the outlines of Branwell's dissolution, a suitably phantom account of the man who painted himself out of his own family portrait." *Village Voice*

ISBN 9780863223631

EVELYN CONLON
Skin of Dreams

"A courageous, intensely imagined and tightly focused book that asks powerful questions of authority . . . this is the kind of Irish novel that is all too rare." Joseph O'Connor

"Astoundingly original . . . a beautiful novel, which will move you by its courage in delving into controversy and its imaginatively spun revelations." *Irish World*

ISBN 9780863223068

MARY ROSE CALLAGHAN

A Bit of a Scandal

"Mary Rose Callaghan hits the nail on the head every time in this sharply observed novel set in the zany world of semi-Bohemian Dublin a generation or two ago. That shabby city of gas meters, broken pay phones, lasagne and cheap wine, is recreated as never before. Young people pursue their heart-breakingly emotional, side-splittingly absurd love affairs in dilapidated bed-sits and seedy pubs, settings that seem as far away as the Middle Ages – which are also evoked, cleverly, in the novel. This is a real tour de force." Éilís Ní Dhuibhne

ISBN 9780863223884 Hardback; 9780863223969 Paperback

MARY ROSE CALLAGHAN

Billy, Come Home

"The slim, moving novel depicts the life of Billy Reilly, a schizophrenic man whose gentle nature and fragile psyche are no match for life in modern Dublin... Without becoming mawkish or preachy, Callaghan delivers an effective indictment of society's failure to care for a vulnerable minority." *Publishers Weekly*

ISBN 9780863223662

MARY ROSE CALLAGHAN

The Visitors' Book

"Callaghan takes the romantic visions some Americans have of Ireland and dismantles them with great comic effect . . . It is near impossible not to find some enjoyment in this book, due to the fully-formed character of Peggy who, with her contrasting vulnerability and searing sarcasm, commands and exerts an irresistible charm." *Sunday Tribune*

ISBN 9780863222801

Marion Urch
An Invitation to Dance

The extraordinary story of a dancer who scandalised the world; a thrilling epic, packed with passionate romance and incident from Ireland to India, from London to Spain, Paris and Munich, from the USA to Australia. This compelling, dramatic work of historical fiction recounts the astonishing life of Lola Montez, a daring young Irish woman who took on the role in life of a Spanish dancer.

ISBN 9780863223839 Hardback; 9780863223952 Paperback

EMER MARTIN
Baby Zero

"An incendiary, thought-provoking novel, like a haunting and spiritual ballad, it moves us and makes us care."
Irvine Welsh

In an unheard of country, each successive Taliban-like regime turns the year back to zero, as if to begin history again. A woman, imprisoned for fighting the fundamentalist government, tells her unborn child the story of three baby zeros – all girls born at times of upheaval.

ISBN 9780863223655

CHET RAYMO
Valentine

"Such nebulous accounts [as we have] have been just waiting for someone to make a work of historical fiction out of them. American novelist and physicist Raymo has duly obliged with his recently published *Valentine: A Love Story*." The Scotsman

"[A] vivid and lively account of how Valentine's life may have unfolded. . . Raymo has produced an imaginative and enjoyable read, sprinkled with plenty of food for philosophical thought." Sunday Tribune

ISBN 9780863223273

PJ CURTIS
The Lightning Tree

"In revealing Mariah's story, Curtis creates an elegiac and moving portrait of Irish rural culture. While the narrative looks backwards over Mariah's extraordinary life, this is also a hugely relevant piece of writing for anyone visiting the region today, as Curtis is highly adept at recreating the mystical and complex atmosphere of life on the Burren, a rugged and wild landscape that remains largely untouched by modern life." *Sunday Telegraph*

ISBN 9780863223471

JOHN B. KEANE
The Bodhrán Makers

The first and best novel from one of Ireland's best-loved writers, a moving and telling portrayal of a rural community in the '50s, a poverty-stricken people who never lost their dignity.

"This powerful and poignant novel provides John B. Keane with a passport to the highest levels of Irish literature." *Irish Press*

ISBN 9780863223006

BRYAN MACMAHON
Hero Town

"For the course of a calendar year, Peter Mulrooney, the musing pedagogue, saunters through the streets and the people, looking at things and leaving them so. They talk to him; he listens, and in his ears we hear the authentic voice of local Ireland, all its tics and phrases and catchcalls. Like Joyce, this wonderful, excellently structured book comes alive when you read it aloud." Frank Delaney, *Sunday Independent*

ISBN 9780863223426

The Novels of Alice Taylor

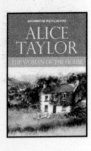

The Woman of the House

"An entrancing story written with much sensitivity and great depth of feeling, this is a delightful read." *Booklist*

"What shines through in *The Woman of the House* is Alice Taylor's love of the Irish countryside and village life of over 40 years ago, its changing seasons and colours, its rhythm and pace." *Irish Independent*

ISBN 9780863222498

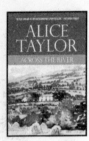

Across the River

"Alice Taylor is an outstanding storyteller. Like a true seanchai, she uses detail to signal twists in the plot or trouble ahead. *Across the River* is the second volume in the saga of the farming Phelans and their neighbours . . . It is tightly plotted fiction, an old-fashioned page-turner with all the moral certainties of a fairy tale." *The Irish Times*

"A master of the genre." *Kirkus Reviews*

ISBN 9780863222856

House of Memories

"It is Alice Taylor's strength to make the natural every-day world come alive in clear fresh prose. In this book, as in her memoirs, she does so beautifully."
The Irish Book Review

"*House of Memories* shows her in her prime as a novelist." *Irish independent*

ISBN 9780863223525

KATE McCAFFERTY

Testimony of an Irish Slave Girl

"A meticulously researched piece of historical fiction that will keep readers both horrified and mesmerized."
Booklist

"Thousands of Irish men, women and children were sold into slavery to work in the sugar-cane fields of Barbados in the 17th century ... McCafferty has researched her theme well and, through Cot, shows us the terrible indignities and suffering endured."
Irish Independent

ISBN 9780863223143 Hardback; 9780863223389 Paperback

J. M. O'Neill

Bennett & Company
Winner of the Kerry Ingredients Book of the Year Award

"O'Neill is in the same fine league as another Irishman with colonial ties, J.G. Farrell – exciting and dangerous, with a touch of the poet." *Sunday Times*

ISBN 9781902011066

J. M. O'Neill

Rellighan, Undertaker

A dark, intriguing modern gothic tale by a novelist who was a master of his craft.

"An uncannily exacting and accomplished novelist."
Observer

ISBN 9780863222603

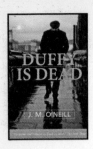

J.M. O Neill
Duffy Is Dead

"A book written sparingly, with wit and without sentimentality, yet the effect can be like poetry ...An exceptional novel." *Guardian*

"Not a single word out of place... Every word of it rings true." *Daily Telegraph*

ISBN 9780863222610

J.M. O Neill
Open Cut

"A hard and squalid world depicted economically and evocatively ... the tension in the slang-spotted dialogue and the mean prose creates effective atmosphere." *Hampstead & Highgate Express*

"A powerful thriller." *Radio Times*

ISBN 9780863222641

Padraic O Farrell
Rebel Heart

A story of Michael Collins, revolutionary leader, the heart and mind of Ireland's struggle for independence.

"I read it in one mid-night sitting; it has the button-holing compulsion of a man met in a dark laneway."
Hugh Leonard

ISBN 9780863222214